ROADS NOT TAKEN

Emily Gallo

Cover design by Raechel Mullen

The author may be reached at ecegallo@gmail.com

ISBN-13: 978-1950561063
ISBN-10: 1545594724

"You miss 100% of the shots you don't take."

Other novels by Emily Gallo:

"The colorful allure of *Venice Beach* is entwined with intrigue and the lives of Emily Gallo's likable characters. The novel has tension, humor, suspense, unique players, unlikely friendships and a fun dose of humanity."

"Jed becomes the focal character in *The Columbarium*, surrounded by Emily Gallo's signature cast of offbeat and compelling characters. Gallo creates a lively and satisfying read in this new novel."

"*Kate and Ruby* is a delicious read, filled with the crazy twists and turns of life. Just as Kate joyfully catapults into retirement, her irascible, former mother-in law Ruby falls into her life again. The fateful interaction between these two women pulled me into each chapter and I could not stop reading."

1

THE CLOUDS STARTED TO ROLL IN. The chill of late afternoon on the beach forced the sun-worshippers to fold up their chairs and blankets. Malcolm took out his phone to check the time. Charlie had promised he'd be back to the table by four so Malcolm would have enough time to shower and dress before he had to be at the restaurant. It was a Monday in March, so the boardwalk wasn't teeming with tourists. And college spring breaks hadn't started yet, so he didn't have to put up with the students' drunken revelry.

"Sorry I'm late," a breathless Charlie rushed up to the table. "We had an emergency at the shelter."

"No problem. What happened?"

"Belligerent husband threatening his frightened wife and kids. So what else is new, right?"

Malcolm shook his head. "Did you have to call the cops?"

"Oh, yeah. That was the only way we could get him to leave. She had a restraining order, but he didn't seem to think it pertained to him even though it had his name on it."

"Did they take him in?"

"For now. We're trying to find a safe house for the wife and kids."

"I better go so I won't be late for work."

"Hey, thanks a lot, Malcolm. You're a godsend. Couldn't do this without you."

Malcolm waved and jogged off. He got home with enough time for a quick shower and he was at the restaurant by five to start his shift. Waiting tables was not his career choice, but it gave him enough to get by until he could figure out whatever the hell his career choice was. He thanked Miss Ruthie every day for leaving him her house, and that it had been paid off for years before he moved into it. Coming up with the taxes and insurance payments a couple of times a year was difficult, but not having to pay rent gave him much needed breathing room. And Venice Beach was a pretty good place to live when you were a black man in your late twenties with no family to rely on.

To say his childhood had been difficult would be an understatement. He was born in

Texas and he and his mother had spent his first fourteen years fleeing from his abusive father. It was the typical story: poverty, alcohol-fueled anger and violence, the son trying to protect his mother and then becoming the target. They moved continually to hide from him and eventually cut off all contact with his mother's family for everyone's protection.

Just when it seemed that they could breathe easy and perhaps lead a normal life, his mother got cancer and was dead within a year. Before becoming too sick to get out of bed, she had worked as a card dealer in a poker club in Inglewood. She had made enough for a one-room apartment in the Oakwood section of Venice, an area that did not cater to tourists and hipsters. It was considered the "ghetto" of Venice although it was still hard to find any apartment under a thousand dollars a month.

Malcolm was fourteen when his mother died. She had finally gone into a coma and spent her last couple of months in the hospital. Malcolm lived alone in the apartment until the landlord found out and then he slept on the boardwalk. His mother had spent her whole life keeping him from that fate. Luckily, she never knew that he had ended up there. And lucky for him, he didn't stay there long, thanks to the homeless resource table he now volunteered at. And thanks to Miss Ruthie who took him in as a foster child and eventually adopted him. And thanks to Jed, a mentor of sorts and a man who touched so many people's lives besides his.

Malcolm had returned to Venice when Miss Ruthie became sick. He was used to caretaking a dying mother and was good at it. His army stint was over by then. It was time to go to school since he had the GI Bill. He could take classes and still nurse Miss Ruthie. She had already found people willing to take the babies into their homes, so Malcolm could devote his time to his studies and to her.

Miss Ruthie had been famous in Los Angeles for taking in newborns of drug-addicted mothers. She had been written up in the Times and interviewed on television. Miss Ruthie took the babies into her home and recruited volunteers to help her rock them in order to quiet their screaming and get them to sleep.

She had been doing this for many years and had gotten enough grant money and private donations to pay off her house. She had started taking in difficult to place foster children as well and had a one hundred percent success rate at finding permanent homes for all her children.

Until she met Malcolm, that is. He was the only one she had adopted herself. They had a special bond from the beginning, and she knew that if she were ever to have had her own child, it would have been someone like Malcolm.

He had acquired some engineering skills in the army, but after Miss Ruthie died, he realized that he was going in that direction to please her, not himself. But he also knew that neither Miss Ruthie nor his mother would have wanted him to spend his life doing something he didn't like.

He had graduated from Santa Monica College in Video Production and done some interning at television stations. He liked his internships at the TV stations, but so far had been unsuccessful in finding a paying job in that field. Consequently, he waited tables at a restaurant appropriately named Cafe Gratitude. He also volunteered at the homeless table and the children's cancer hospital: his way of honoring both his mother and Miss Ruthie, and Jed.

Malcolm arrived at the restaurant a little before five to find it packed with Happy Hour patrons. The Venice Cafe Gratitude was one of several in California. It served gourmet, organic, vegan/vegetarian food and was expensive. He had known little about gourmet vegetarian food when he applied for the job. As a child he had eaten whatever was cheap, and his army stint had hardly been a gastronomic learning experience. But he was extremely personable, a quick learner, and skilled at pretending to know things.

The restaurant catered to the locals who cared about where their food came from. Tips were good, and he was able to pay for the essentials, but he wanted a car, so he had decided it was time to look for a daytime job as well. He probably could have expanded his hours at the restaurant to include lunch, but he wanted something completely different. He had noticed a Help Wanted sign on the outside of one of the buildings on the boardwalk and planned to stop there in the morning.

The evening went quickly. The Happy Hour crowd went home and was replaced by a busy dinner throng of "grateful" customers. Malcolm left the restaurant with a healthy sum, half of which he planned to deposit into his savings account.

He always felt a little uneasy walking home from work carrying his tip money. It was late and the most direct route took him through the seedier part of Venice. He often went several blocks out of his way to walk home on the boardwalk. At night the sleeping homeless took over the benches and the openings between buildings. The teenage meth heads were still active, but there was a visible police presence. Most of all, he liked to end his workday listening to the waves and absorbing the negative ions from the ocean.

The Help Wanted sign was on one of the buildings closest to the Santa Monica side of the boardwalk. It was a residential building that stood out because it was at least three times larger than its surrounding structures. There was no other information on the sign, so he made a mental note to stop by the next day.

2

ALTHOUGH MALCOLM'S DAYS WERE SIMPLE AND QUIET, HIS NIGHTS WERE NOT ALWAYS THAT WAY. Insomnia and nightmares were frequent visitors to his bed. He couldn't escape his traumatic childhood totally unscathed, no matter how hard he tried. He hid it well, though, with a calm, happy-go-lucky demeanor.

His attendance record at school had been spotty, due to his constant moving around. When his mother got ill, he stopped going to school altogether because he was afraid to leave her alone. But she made sure that he had a library card every place they lived and the library became his refuge. He had a natural ability in math and science, and managed to pass the high school qualifying exams with flying colors, even though he hadn't had any of the prerequisites. And once he started living with Miss Ruthie, she made sure he attended school and his academic progress accelerated.

The army was thrilled to have him enlist and put him in the engineering program.

Malcolm tossed and turned until he finally got out of bed at eight, after giving up on getting back to sleep. He showered and dressed, and grabbed a donut and coffee on the boardwalk before making his way up to the building with the Help Wanted sign. It was a residence for low income, section 8 seniors and was clean, attractive and well maintained. Its location also made it extremely desirable, so its waiting list was long.

Malcolm walked through the front door and found himself in a bright, airy lobby with a counter on his left and an elevator on his right. In front of him was a huge community room with every comfort and convenience that included an upright piano and a large flat screen television. A bell rang as Malcolm came through the door and a person came out of a back office.

"Hello. May I help you?"

"Uh, yes." Malcolm stumbled through his answer. He was trying to identify whether this person was male or female. He/she was dressed in jeans and a T-shirt with longish hair, and had well-defined muscles, but not necessarily in a masculine way. He checked for an Adam's apple but couldn't tell if one was there or not. "I'm here about the Help Wanted sign in the window?"

"Okay." He/she took a piece of paper out of a drawer and handed it to Malcolm. "Here's an application." The voice was low.

"What exactly is the job?" he asked.

"Activities Coordinator."

"Oh. Well, what qualifications would I need?"

He/she shrugged. "Just fill out the application and don't worry about it."

Malcolm was perplexed, but figured why not? Why should he care? How hard could the job be? "I just wanted to make sure I didn't need some kind of medical background or something."

"Nah. You'd just be in charge of the fun and games. Anyway, there's a director who figures it out. You'd be the guy making it happen."

Malcolm wasn't sure what to make of this person. Was it sarcasm or indifference? Or both? "Okay. Can I sit in that room to fill it out?"

"Doesn't matter to me where you sit."

Now Malcolm was getting the picture. This person did not like their job. It was indifference. "Do you have a pen?"

"Here."

Malcolm took the pen and the application into the community room and sat down. It was too late for breakfast and too early for lunch. There was just a smattering of residents sitting on the sofas and chairs and they seemed oblivious and disinterested. The television was on, but no one seemed to be watching. A couple of them were reading, but most were just sitting and staring into space.

It didn't take long for Malcolm to finish filling out the application. It was pretty generic with basic questions about education and past employment and names of a couple of references. He added his volunteer experience working at the homeless table and the pediatric hospital. It never hurts to pad the resume, he was always told. "Here you go." He handed the application back.

"I'll give it to the director and she'll call you."

And at that, Malcolm turned around and walked back through the door onto the boardwalk, ten minutes after he arrived. He didn't have much more knowledge about the job than he had before, but he felt pretty confident that he could do this job easily. It would be pretty cushy and that's exactly what he needed right now.

He went home to check Craigslist and LinkedIn for any jobs. He still had some of his television contacts and thought about giving them a call too. But he soon found himself wandering off the jobs listing web pages to search for activity coordinator salaries and job descriptions. Something definitely interested him about this job. Maybe it was just that it was new and different. Maybe there was something appealing about working with old people as opposed to the entitled, arrogant hipsters in the entertainment industry and the restaurant employees who all wanted to be doing something else. He closed his eyes and leaned back in his chair to ponder that, and was asleep in less than a minute. He had mastered the art of sleeping in weird positions in the army. It was a skill he had to master if he was ever going to get any sleep at all.

The ringing and vibrating of his phone jarred him awake. He took it out of his pocket, didn't recognize the number and was about to wait for the message, but decided to answer. "Hello?"

"Malcolm Washington?"

"Speaking."

"My name is Annabel Lee. I am the director of Marie Moss Senior Housing. You applied for a job?"

"Yes. That was quick!"

She laughed. "We need someone right away. The last person who had the job left unexpectedly, so we need to fill it as soon as possible."

Malcolm wondered why the person left unexpectedly. Was the job that bad or was it a personal reason? Obviously he couldn't ask, but luckily she answered anyway. "Nothing to do with the job. Family emergency."

"I guess I was curious."

"Can you come back this morning for an interview?"

"Sure." Why would they need an activity coordinator so desperately? The old people couldn't play cards without someone watching them? It was a residence, not a nursing home for Alzheimer's patients. "I can be there in half an hour."

"Perfect. Just tell Savali to page me when you get there. I actually oversee several places and I'm not at the Moss House right now, but I can be there a few minutes after I get the page."

"Savali?"

"I believe it was Savali who took your application?"

"Oh yes." Damn. Knowing the name of the person didn't help Malcolm know the gender.

"Okay. See you soon."

Malcolm went to his closet to take out his nice slacks and blazer and realized he probably didn't need to wear them for this job. But he kind of liked getting dressed up and didn't get many opportunities. As he dressed, he tried to remember why the director's name sounded so familiar. Annabel Lee. Oh yeah. A poem. He quickly took out his phone and looked it up. Edgar Allan Poe. He learned it in his high school English class with Miss McGee. It was about the death of a beautiful woman in a kingdom by the sea and how they would be reunited. He smiled remembering those days in high school . . . and the women whose deaths he has grieved.

3

SAVALI GREETED MALCOLM WITH A SMILE AND A HIGH FIVE WHEN HE ENTERED THE LOBBY TO MEET WITH ANNABEL LEE. "I wanted someone more my age to work with so I put in a good word for you," Savali explained.

Malcolm laughed. "Thanks."

"She's not here yet but she's on her way."

Savali was much friendlier than when he came in earlier that day. He wasn't sure what to make of it. Maybe it was something he'd put on his application. "No problem. I'll just take a look around." He went into the community room to see if there were more people, or at least a different group, partaking of the offerings. He saw the same few catatonic chair warmers, but there were also a couple of gentlemen watching a baseball game on television. "So who's winning?" Malcolm asked.

"This year? It's always the other guys," one of the men answered, scowling.

Before Malcolm had a chance to answer him, a middle-aged Asian woman in business attire appeared at his side. "Malcolm? I'm Annabel."

"Hi," he replied.

"Let's go into my office."

The men watching television never averted their eyes from the screen and continued to grouse and grumble about their lousy team. Malcolm assumed it was the Dodgers since they were in Los Angeles, but he knew that many people came to Venice from other places. It was quite possible that they were Chicago Cubs fans and those fans had plenty to complain about, at least they used to until the Cubs finally won the World Series after a 108-year drought.

"Sorry about the mess in here," Annabel said as they entered her office. Malcolm looked around and found very little out of place. Apparently, Annabel liked perfection. In fact, he figured the best thing would be to say nothing. He just sat down quietly and waited for her to do the talking. "Thanks for coming in on such short notice," she continued as they sat across from each other. She took his application off the desk and scanned it. "I haven't had a chance to look at this yet. Savali just called me and said that you were one that I shouldn't let get away."

"Wow. I'll have to be sure and thank him, uh her, uh Savali."

"I see that you've been in the army, worked in television, and volunteered with the homeless and with sick children. But have you ever worked with the elderly?"

"I took care of my foster mother at the end of her life."

"You wait tables at Cafe Gratitude. So you know about food?"

"I guess." He wasn't sure what to make of all this. He felt like it was a bit of a stretch to assume that he knew much about nursing the elderly or about diet and nutrition from his experiences, but if she wanted to make the connections, who was he to stop her. "So what exactly is the job? I'm still unclear."

Annabel sat back in her chair and smiled at him. "This is a residence for low income seniors. It is not a nursing home or an assisted living facility. It's an apartment building for people over sixty-two. We don't offer medical assistance, housekeeping or transportation services. Some people living here have home health aides that come during the day but don't spend the night. We don't offer classes or arts and crafts type activities, but we have a computer room and a community room for the residents to use. We just need someone to monitor and help the residents. It's more about having a rudimentary knowledge of computers, being able to plan and help when we have events and well, basically just being personable."

Malcolm smiled. "I'm pretty sure I can handle all that."

"Yes. I have no doubt that you could."

"What are the hours? I work at the cafe five nights a week."

"What time do you have to be there?"

"Five."

"We can work around that. The only problems would arise if we have a party or event scheduled, but that is a pretty rare occurrence."

"If I know enough ahead of time I can always trade with someone if I'm scheduled to work that night."

"That sounds good. I just need to make some calls to check your references and then fill out some paperwork. I'll call you this afternoon. I'm sure Savali will be very happy."

Malcolm was dying to ask Annabel what Savali's gender was. He was hoping she would refer to her with a "he" or a "she" and racked his brain trying to find an appropriate way to get her to spill the beans. But Annabel stood and opened the door to her office. The interview was over. "Thanks," he said. "I'll wait to hear from you. Do you mind if I look around?"

"Sure. Ask Savali to show you."

Malcolm walked out and stuck his head into the back office where Savali was typing on a computer. "Hi. Annabel said I should ask you to show me around."

"Awesome. So you're gonna start working here?"

"I think so. She needs to check my references and complete some forms. She's going to call me later, but I doubt there will be any problems."

"Let's go." Savali stood and took Malcolm's arm. He welcomed the change in her manner. "You're going to find some of the residents are fun and interesting, but there are a lot of old fogies who are negative about everything. I just try to ignore them."

"They're just a microcosm of the larger population."

"Microcosm huh? Hmmm. Big word for a waiter."

"I'm a regular walking dictionary."

"Ha! And a comedian too."

"Not really. What about you? Now that you've read my resume, you know all about me. What's your story?"

"Born in Samoa. Moved here when I was a kid."

"Here being America or Venice Beach?"

"I've been in Venice for something like fifteen years. Hey Nick!" Savali called out to a man coming down the hall. "This is Malcolm. He works here now."

"Nice to meet you, Nick," Malcolm responded.

"Yeah, yeah, yeah," Nick waved his hand as he walked off.

"Nick's one of the cool ones. He's a grouch but he's funny."

"By the way, you probably shouldn't be introducing me as someone who works here. I haven't gotten the final okay from Annabel yet."

"You have the job. She always listens to me."

Savali steered him toward two tables with three computers on each. They were older models of desktop PCs with an ancient printer and a tangle of wires covering the middle of the table and the floor. "Do these all work?"

Savali shrugged. "That will be up to you to figure out. Some of them do. I think the printer is on its last legs though."

They saw the same guys watching the ball game and a few others wandering around aimlessly. "Do they stay around here mostly?" Malcolm asked.

"It varies. There's some you hardly ever see, the ones with family and friends. But there are some who don't seem to have anywhere to go."

"By the way, I need to thank you for the endorsement."

"I've got good instincts. See ya, Malcolm." Savali was gone before he had a chance to answer. He watched her walk back to the office and tried to decipher her gender from her gait but without much luck.

4

MALCOLM WASN'T SURE HOW HE FELT ABOUT THE PLACE OR THE JOB. Savali seemed like a good co-worker and Annabel was hardly ever there. He always felt more comfortable when the boss wasn't around much. But he still didn't understand what the job would entail. He spent the afternoon scanning employment websites and Craigslist but had to admit that nothing jumped out at him. This job would be an easy walk to and from home and to and from the cafe. It might be a good way to earn some money while he decided what to do as a career and it would help toward purchasing that car. He wouldn't have much invested in it and he could quit without feeling guilty.

He started a search for used cars. Now he was really letting his daydreaming take over. He had a long way to go before he would have enough saved up, but working two jobs would speed him towards his goal while giving him less time to spend.

He found himself searching for vans and campers and wound up on a page listing old VW buses from the seventies. At first he felt like a fool. It was such a cliché to look for such an iconic symbolic car. But they were so cool! Their prices ran the gamut too. He found several in the $10,000 range, but there were also some selling for $90,000. Maybe if he restored it to its original condition. But what was he talking about! He wasn't a car guy and wasn't interested in becoming one. Luckily for him, his phone rang.

"Hello? Oh, hi Miss Lee."

"Malcolm, I've called the cafe and the homeless shelter, and they both had nothing but praise for you. I'd like to offer you the job."

"Okay. By the way, we didn't talk about salary and how many hours a week."

"Let's say nine to four. Will that give you enough time to get to your evening job?"

Malcolm thought for a minute and calculated the time for walking and showering and getting dressed. "Yeah. That would work."

"Twelve an hour to start." Malcolm was silent. "I'm sorry but that's the best I can do."

"Can I think about it?"

"It will be an easy job for you and we can be flexible with your hours."

"I know." She was right. And what did he expect for a salary? He thought again about working more hours at the restaurant and how much more he could earn with tips. But this would be a steady salary that he could count on. And it wouldn't be tiring. "Okay. I'll take it."

"Wonderful. When would you like to start? There's some paperwork you need to sign."

"I could come in tomorrow and sign the papers and then start Monday. It is a Monday through Friday job, right?"

"Yes. Just let me know what time you'll be coming in. I have meetings all morning, but anytime in the afternoon."

"I'll come on my way to work. Four?"

"Fine. I'll see you then. And call me Annabel."

"Okay. Thanks." He hung up and went back to his computer. He still had a little time before he had to go to work. He went back to the trucks/vans for sale page and let his mind wander.

It was a busy night at the restaurant. Malcolm wasn't sure why. Thursdays were not usually his night to work. He had agreed to take on an extra shift. He was one of the few people who didn't have much else to do and was willing to work as much as he could.

He approached a table that had just been seated. The couple was dressed fashionably and in fancier attire than the usual Cafe customers. They were both attractive, he in a rugged way with an athletic build. Her body was muscular, but her face and dress were feminine and sensual. Savali looked up at him and grinned, a childlike twinkle in her eye. "Hi Malcolm."

He almost dropped his tray. "Savali?"

"Yep. This is Byron. And this is Malcolm." The men shook hands. "I wasn't sure if you were working tonight. Byron wanted to go somewhere more upscale, but I talked him into coming here."

Malcolm was still in shock, seeing Savali dressed up as a woman. He hadn't been sure what her gender was, but he had been leaning toward male. He still wasn't sure and found it hard to answer as he racked his brain trying to make sense of what he was seeing.

"Do you serve drinks?" Byron asked, breaking the spell.

"Uh, just beer and wine. They're listed on the back of the menu." Malcolm finally found his tongue.

Savali was still grinning, relishing every moment of Malcolm's confusion. "Thanks. So Annabel tells me that you took the job."

"Uh, yeah." He took a deep breath. "I'll be right back to take your order." He left hurriedly, practically running into the kitchen. He leaned against the wall, watching the other servers bustle about.

"You okay, Malcolm?" one of the servers asked.

"Yeah I'm fine." He smiled self-consciously. He was usually the picture of the cool, calm and collected waiter. He was good at his job, knowing exactly when to appear at a table without being overly attentive. Savali, all dressed up as a woman, had really thrown him for a loop. It wasn't even so much that Savali was perhaps a she, or that she might be a drag queen. It was how beautiful and feminine she looked. And how attracted he had been to her. He took another deep breath and went back out to the main dining room to attend to his customers.

"We'll have a bottle of the Pinot Noir from Chile," Byron said pompously to Malcolm as he approached their table.

"Excellent choice." Malcolm wasn't going to let Byron act like he knew more about wine than he did. Was he really competing with this guy for Savali's attention? "I'll get the wine and be back for your order." He left hastily, without his usually cool, professional demeanor.

Malcolm tried to give good service to all his tables while sneaking glances at Savali and Byron. They seemed to laugh a lot more and louder as the wine bottle emptied. He watched to see if they also got affectionate. Thankfully that didn't happen, but they certainly seemed to enjoy each other's company. Byron was a good tipper. Apparently, he hadn't noticed Malcolm showing an interest in his date.

"Thanks for the great service, Malcolm. And tell the chef the food was delicious." Savali grinned and Malcolm tried to detect if it was meant sarcastically.

"Thanks for coming in." He smiled back. He really was glad she had come in. At least he now knew he could call her "she" without offense, even if she was a he. He watched them leave and took a peek out the window to see if Byron put his arm around her or took her hand. He did neither. Malcolm felt relieved that they had left, and he could concentrate on his other tables.

The rest of the evening went quickly, and he had ended up with a good take. The servers sat around a table counting their tips and compensating the bussers, drinking the bottles of wine that customers had left unfinished on their tables. "We're heading over to The Brig for a drink. Want to come?" one of the servers asked Malcolm.

This was not something he usually did. He just wasn't that much of a partier or a drinker. But he thought that it might be one of the last nights he'd be able to stay out late since he was starting the new job on Monday. And on the weekend, his job ended later and the bars in Venice were lively and crowded. "Sure," he answered. He could use a little decompressing. Savali's coming out (if that's what one called it) threw him for a loop. But what really shocked him was his attraction to her.

5

MALCOLM ENDED UP STAYING WITH A FEW OF THE SERVERS UNTIL LAST CALL AT 2 AM. It was hip-hop night, so he danced most of the time. That meant he didn't drink as much as some of the others. He made up for that by going back to one of the servers apartments and sharing some weed. He went home when they started doing lines of cocaine.

Malcolm fell into bed at four and slept straight through until noon. He hadn't had a night like that since before Miss Ruthie died. He had gotten most of those kinds of nights out of his system when he was in college, in the army and working in Hollywood. Taking care of Miss Ruthie had reminded him how bad things were before she had adopted him. He never wanted that life again of being on the run and living in fleabag apartments, and then being homeless. And truthfully, he had never found drinking and taking drugs to be all that much fun.

He got up leisurely and spent the early part of the afternoon looking at cars on Craigslist. He still found himself gravitating toward the trucks and vans, but at least he had moved away from the old VWs. He wasn't sure why. It was probably more prudent to be looking for small cars; something easier to park and good on gas made much more sense in Los Angeles. Maybe he should be looking at a small SUV. None of this really mattered since he was far from having a decent amount to spend.

It was soon time to shower and dress and stop off to sign the papers. He was conflicted on how he felt about seeing Savali after their encounter last night. Her dress at the senior residence could be described as unisex yet the night before she was the picture of sensual femininity. He knew that she was quite aware of how she looked, and how she made him feel. That embarrassed him and he was beginning to feel that maybe it wasn't a good idea for him to work there. First of all, he still wasn't sure what gender she was physically and wasn't interested in a sexual relationship with a man. Secondly, if she was a female anatomically, it was never a good idea to have a romantic relationship at your job. Yet he liked her and wanted to know her better.

Savali wasn't at the reception area when he got there, thankfully. Annabel was waiting for him, so he was able to sign the papers quickly and be out of there before Savali showed up. He wondered if she was purposefully avoiding him.

The night was busy; Fridays usually were. He had enough seniority at the cafe to get the weekend shifts. He also got his choice of weekday nights and often he made more tips on a Tuesday than on a Saturday. On Mondays and Tuesdays he would often be the only server on, so if it got busy, the customers would feel sorry to see him rushing around and tipped especially well. He actually enjoyed waiting tables. Most customers at Cafe Gratitude were friendly and knew how to tip.

His weekends were usually filled with his volunteer work. He didn't have a regular schedule at the hospital. He just showed up and visited with the children whose parents weren't there. Some of the kids lived far from the hospital and their parents had to work or take care of other siblings at home so could only come sporadically. But then there were a few who had no one. They were the ones who came from foster homes and they were the ones Malcolm focused on. Sometimes he brought them gifts, but mostly they just wanted his company and his caring. He could provide that easily and honestly. The hardest part was losing them. That happened way too often.

He did keep a schedule for manning the homeless table. Charlie had appointments with companies and nonprofits that donated food, toiletries, clothing and money. He tried to make them as regular as possible so Malcolm would know when he needed to be at the table every week. Things would have to change now that Malcolm wouldn't be available during the day Monday through Friday, but Charlie would figure out a way to make it work. Malcolm could step up his time on the weekends.

He spent Saturday and often Sunday mornings working at the homeless table. The population had its share of regulars and long timers, many of them homeless by choice. There were, as always, those who were mentally ill and/or addicts. But lately there were more of the type who had never thought they would wind up in this situation. Those were the saddest group. Loss of employment, medical bills, divorce or death had put them out on the streets.

Saturday and Sunday afternoons he was at the children's cancer hospital. He played with the kids, read to them, and took them for walks down the corridors. But sometimes they were too sick to do anything but stay in bed, so Malcolm just sat with them, silently holding their hands.

Malcolm had long ago pushed aside any need for having social activities. He kept busy with these pursuits rather than face his loneliness. He had always been sought after for friendship, but when he never reciprocated, people stopped trying. Once in a while he would go out with coworkers like he had the other night. That was his way of staying under the radar. He had learned that skill in the army and the entertainment business.

6

MALCOLM WOKE UP EARLY MONDAY MORNING, APPREHENSIVE BUT ALSO EXCITED ABOUT HIS FIRST DAY ON THE JOB. He was more nervous about seeing Savali than about the job itself. He wondered how she'd be dressed and whether she had picked up on his attraction to her. He had no idea what his job entailed, who would train him if anyone, who he answered to, or exactly what he was supposed to do for six hours every day. He wasn't concerned, though. He was sure he could wing it. How hard could it be to keep some elderly people busy when they all seemed to have nothing much else to do? He assumed Annabel would be there when he got to Moss House and could at least give him some direction. Then he remembered that Savali said there was a director who planned the activities. Hopefully, the director would be there.

He got to the front door of the building before nine and went inside. Savali stood at the counter helping one of the residents figure out how to answer a text message on her iPhone. When Savali saw Malcolm walk in, she smiled and winked. "Here's just the guy to help you. Malcolm, this is Violet. She just got an iPhone and needs help."

Malcolm took the iPhone from Savali. "How do you do, Violet. It's nice to meet you."

"Well listen to him. Ain't he the polite one." Violet's southern accent was strong.

"Let's go to the community room and sit down, and I can help you navigate this phone."

Violet fluttered her eyes at Malcolm demurely. "Oh my, yes. Let's."

Savali laughed loudly and imitated Violet's flirtatious come-on. "Oh Malcolm!"

Malcolm smiled at Savali and took Violet's arm. He was actually glad that Violet had been there to diffuse any sexual tension in the air. Savali was back to her uniform of unisex clothing, so it wasn't hard to do.

Malcolm took the phone and sat on the sofa. Violet sat down next to him, her leg right up against his. "You see this icon up here in the left hand corner? This is for texting. Just press it and put in the phone number of the person you want to message."

"Okay. Then what?"

"Here's the keyboard. Just type the message."

"You know, I never learned to type. I didn't have to work like some other girls. I always had a man taking care of me."

"You were very lucky, then."

"Oh yes, there was always one in the wings, just waiting for me to beckon him in."

"It just takes practice."

"Oh yes it does. I know exactly how to get a man's attention and then keep it. Did you know I was in beauty pageants before I could walk?"

"I meant the typing," Malcolm said with a sigh.

Violet shrugged and took the phone. "Let's see if I can figure this out."

Malcolm thought this might be something he could do with the others. Probably helping the residents with their smart phones and computers would be a good activity. Maybe he should make it a weekly "class." Violet was in no hurry to leave Malcolm even though he was done, so he thought he needed to be the one to get up and leave the table. He went back to the reception area to see if anyone was showing up to give him an inkling of what he was supposed to do in this job. Maybe at the very least, there were some written directions or a job description.

"Hey Savali. Is Annabel coming to show me the ropes?"

"No idea, big guy."

"Well, could you call her?"

She dialed a number and all the while she was talking, she never took her eyes off of Malcolm. "Malcolm's here and wants to know what his job description is. Okay. I'll tell him." She hung up. "She said she'd be here in about half an hour, and you should introduce yourself to some of the residents."

Malcolm stared at Savali for a minute, trying to understand why this whole thing was so casual and haphazard. "Well, what did the person do before me? When did they leave?"

"I don't know. It's been awhile, a long while. What do you care, anyway? Just make it up as you go along. The people living here don't care what you do."

"Then why was I hired?"

"Truth?"

"Yeah."

"I think there was some stipulation or something that there was supposed to be an activities coordinator because they were getting some kind of grant.”

“Huh? So was there ever someone else doing this job?”

“Not since I’ve been here.”

“So basically, it doesn’t matter what I do as long as they have a body on paper being paid out of this grant money?”

“Something like that. But hey, it’ll be a nice cushy job.” Savali grinned.

“I guess.” He turned around abruptly and went back into the community room. He was a little angry about the whole thing, but he’d see what Annabel had to say when she got there. He looked around and saw a handful of people reading newspapers and playing cards. A game show was on TV, but no one was watching it. Violet was sitting at the table where two men were playing cards, flirting and trying to divert their attention away from the hands they were holding. They seemed less than interested in her. Apparently she flirted with everyone, and these men were probably tired of it. Malcolm walked over to meet them. “Hello, my name is Malcolm. I’ll be working here now.” He extended his hand. Neither of them offered their hands back or their names.

"Malcolm just showed me how to text on my iPhone," Violet offered. "He's such a dear to help me."

The men just nodded and continued to concentrate on their cards. "Hah! Gin!" One of the men lay his hand down with a flourish. The other one threw his cards down in disgust.

"Nice hand." Malcolm was still trying to engage them somehow. "What are your names?" He had finally decided to just ask.

"Phil. This is Les. He's a sucker. Can't play gin to save his life, but he keeps pretending."

"Oh shut up." Les stood and left the table.

"Don't mind him," Violet added. "Les doesn't like that he loses all the time. He's a nice guy when he's not playing cards."

Malcolm shook his head and glanced over at the two or three people reading and walked over to them. They were a bit more accommodating and polite, so he felt a little better about the prospects of keeping this job. He shot the breeze with them and finally Annabel arrived and brought him back to her office. "I'm sorry I'm late. I had an emergency over at one of my other properties."

"No problem. I'm just a bit confused about what this job actually entails."

"Well, we haven't actually ever had an activities coordinator here. We've had an activities director over all the properties we manage here in the Los Angeles area, but most of the other ones are bigger and have more amenities. The director hasn't paid much attention to this one. That's why we thought we needed an onsite person to run things."

"So what things should I be running?" Malcolm looked around. "I don't think they need help reading, watching television, or playing cards."

"Well, that's what I hope you'll come up with: new things for them to do."

Apparently, she was not going to share with him what Savali had told him, that it was a job mostly in name. "Well, I did help Violet with her phone. I had thought maybe some kind of computer and smart phone class or something."

"That's perfect. Whatever you come up with. Just talk to them and see what they want. They'll be happy to complain to you about what they feel they're lacking here."

Malcolm couldn't help but laugh. "You're probably right. Well, do you think I could also talk to the director and see what he has come up with?"

"Sure. I'll have him send you an email or call you." She stood and Malcolm took it as a signal that she was done with him. He glanced up at the clock on the wall and saw that he still had several hours to kill until his first day on the job was over.

7

MALCOLM DECIDED TO GET A LIST OF ALL THE RESIDENTS NAMES FROM SAVALI. He would go around and take pictures and then he could put names and faces together. He would learn who everyone was. If he memorized everyone's name, they might be more likely to talk to him. So far, other than Violet, the residents were aloof, some almost bordering on hostile.

He got the list from Savali and started off on his mission. Violet, of course, loved having her picture taken and posed as seductively as a woman in her eighties could. Nick entered the lobby on his way out the door and downright refused to have his picture taken.

"It's only for me. I'm not going to post it anywhere. I just want to learn everyone's name." Malcolm asked several times, but Nick was adamant and left the building, grumbling to himself. Malcolm caught a few people in the community room. They weren't enthusiastic, but at least they didn't flat out refuse like Nick. He decided to knock on doors to introduce himself and to take their pictures. Most people were home and agreeable. A few even responded like Violet, enthusiastic and even excited about it. Malcolm guessed those were the lonelier ones who had few visitors and not much to do or many places to go.

It took the morning and into the afternoon to get everyone's pictures. When he got back to the reception desk, Savali wasn't there and there was a sign on the counter that said she would be back later. Malcolm looked around and saw no one taking her place at the counter. He wondered how they managed. What if someone came in or called? Was there a maintenance person around? Before he thought about that too long, a janitor came in from the community room. "You must be Malcolm. Savali told me you were starting today."

A man smiled at him. He was small and wiry, and not much younger than most of the residents. He was dressed in a gray uniform with the name "Jose" printed on his shirt. Malcolm shook his hand. "Nice to meet you, is it Jose?"

The man laughed. "Si senor — very observant." Malcolm smiled. Apparently Jose had Savali's dry sense of humor. "Do you need anything?"

Malcolm laughed back. "Yeah, maybe a job description."

"No such thing in this place. You just play it by ear and make it up as you go along. That's what both Savali and I do."

Malcolm laughed. "I guess that's true." He was getting hungry but figured he should wait for Savali before going out to get something to eat. He checked his phone for a call or email from the so-called activities director, although he was starting to wonder if that person even existed. Maybe it was just a ploy to make the whole thing seem real. He sat down with the photos and the list, checking off the ones he had and marking the names of the people he still had to get pictures of.

Savali came back with two shopping bags from high-end boutiques on Abbot Kinney Boulevard, one in each hand. Malcolm's curiosity about her was piqued again. She was an enigma, no doubt about it. "Shopping, I see." Malcolm felt the need to say something and that's what popped into his head, ridiculous as it sounded.

"Very perceptive."

"Yes, one of my finest qualities."

"Did you get some lunch?" she asked.

"I was waiting for you to get back."

She grinned. "To take me to lunch?"

"No. I just thought one of us should be here."

"Aren't you the responsible one. Go ahead and get some lunch. I won't be watching the clock. Take as long as you want."

Malcolm shook his head and left the building. Savali's sarcasm was actually starting to get on his nerves. He walked down the boardwalk, trying to decide what he wanted to eat. There wasn't that much on the boardwalk that one could categorize as healthy, so he wound up with a piece of pizza and went to the beach to eat it. He returned in less than half an hour and went immediately back to work, knocking on the doors of the people who either hadn't been home earlier or hadn't opened their doors.

He took a few more pictures and sat down at a table in the community room to sort through them and memorize names. The ball game was on, and the same couple of guys who had been watching it the other day were there. This time Malcolm called them by name and sat and schmoozed for a while. They were joined by a couple of other residents, and it turned out

49

to be time well spent. Malcolm asked them what they might like to see as activities available to them and they had some suggestions. At least it started out that way. "How about having a drama class? Didn't you used to work in Hollywood, Malcolm?" one of the writing teachers asked.

"I was a cameraman, not an actor. But that's a good idea. I'm sure there are people here who have some acting experience." Malcolm wrote that down.

"Singing too?" another resident asked.

"Good idea."

"We need a snack machine and a soda machine." Joseph added.

"What are we, a motel? Next thing you'll want an ice machine!" George muttered.

After a few minutes it turned into more of a complaint fest, just as Annabel had predicted. They grumbled about things they'd like to see changed at the residence.

"Where's the paint job they promised for my apartment when I moved in? I've been here eight years and they said they'd paint every seven years!" another resident griped.

"Yeah. And then there's the garbage collection. It gets too full to be picked up only once a week. We need it done twice a week."

Malcolm wrote them down, too. He might as well be on their side and advocate for them if necessary.

He played some cards and watched some television to pass the time. He checked his phone several times to see if the so-called director had sent him an email or called, but nothing. He also glanced over to the lobby to check on Savali, but she seemed busy with some kind of paperwork. At four he told the "guys and gals" that he'd see them tomorrow and went to the front desk. Savali was in the back office, so he called out to her, "I'll see you tomorrow," and left.

His evening at work was uneventful. The tips were fine, but business was on the slow side so he decided to let one of the other servers stay on late this time. Usually he was the one who offered, but now that he was working two jobs, he figured he could use the down time. He was in bed by ten and asleep five minutes later. He slept fitfully, though, trying to make sense of his new job and his new acquaintances. He woke up the next morning just as perplexed as he was the day before.

8

MALCOLM WEAVED HIS WAY THROUGH THE EARLY MORNING MAZE OF EXERCISE FANATICS. There were joggers, speed walkers, bicyclists, rollerbladers, skateboarders, and even some of the new fitness craze: crawlers. He threaded through the long line at Charlie's table to say hello and tell him about his new job and what hours he would now be available. There weren't a lot of tourists on the boardwalk this early, so Charlie's table was one of the few set up. The political activists, entertainers, and merchants didn't get there until after ten.

He arrived at the Moss House right on time and found, once again, no one there but Savali. "Good morning," he nodded to her as he walked briskly by the desk.

"Where's the fire?" she answered.

"What do you mean?"

"You seem to be in a big hurry. Hot date?"

"No," Malcolm snapped. "What time do you get here?"

"When I finish my workout," Savali answered, coolly. "It doesn't matter, you know, when either of us gets here. No one's gonna notice."

"Don't you have to be open certain hours to answer phones or anything?"

"How often have you heard the phone ring?"

"I guess I haven't. What workout do you do?"

"I go to Muscle Beach. I have a regular routine."

"Oh yeah? Bodybuilding?" Malcolm asked.

She batted her eyelashes and tilted her head. "Do you like what you see?"

Malcolm turned abruptly and walked back to the community room. He didn't think her last question needed an answer. She knew damn well what she was doing to him.

Violet came rushing over to him as he entered the room. "Oh Malcolm." She hugged him like he was her long lost grandson. "You missed all the excitement."

"What happened?" he said, squirming out of her tight grip.

"There was a fight. George and Nick went at it."

"When? This morning?"

"Last night. In the hallway."

"Why? What were they fighting about?"

"I don't know. It wasn't me. I haven't been with either of them for some time now."

Malcolm looked at her warily. He doubted she had ever been with either of them. He had already decided that she was living in her own universe. "Well, what happened?"

"Some of the fellas stopped them before either of them got too beat up."

"Maybe I'll go check on them." He remembered where Nick's apartment was but wasn't sure about George's. He had to work a little at even remembering who George was, but thought he might be one of the baseball fans. Nick's apartment was on the second floor. The elevator was right by the community room, but Malcolm preferred the stairs. Most people took the elevator, so he wouldn't run into anyone on the stairs. That's the way he preferred it after his last encounter with Savali. He needed to get back into his cool, calm, collected mode. He couldn't believe how flustered she could make him feel.

He knocked on Nick's door and waited for him to open it. He could hear him grunting and cursing. Finally Nick opened the door, dressed in a tattered bathrobe. "What the hell do you want?" Nick groused.

"I heard you were in a fight. I wanted to make sure you were okay."

"So now you know. I'm fine. Take a hike." Nick started to close the door, but Malcolm put his foot in it.

"Hold on. I think my job is to keep the peace in our little community, so can you tell me what the problem was?"

"You a cop?" Nick asked warily.

"No."

"Then what the hell are you?"

"I'm, uh, activities coordinator."

"So go coordinate some activities and leave me alone. And get your foot out of my door."

Malcolm removed his foot and Nick slammed the door. "Could you tell me what apartment George lives in?" Malcolm shouted. Not surprisingly, there was no response. Malcolm turned around and started back to the staircase. He was almost knocked over by a man with a gray ponytail down his back. He had a long gray beard almost as long down the front of him. He tottered down the hall, holding onto the walls to keep from falling. Malcolm figured he was drunk, but he didn't smell of alcohol. He took the man's arm. "Can I help you?"

"I forgot my cane. Could you go back to my room and get it for me?" He leaned against the wall and his shaking hand reached into his pocket to retrieve a set of keys. He painstakingly went through the set until he came to a specific one and handed it to Malcolm. "It's last door on the left."

Malcolm took the keys and went to the man's apartment. He opened the door and stepped inside. There wasn't much furniture and it was pushed against the walls except for one chair placed directly in front of an old, small television. The cane was next to this chair. He picked it up and locked the apartment and returned to the hallway. He gave the man the keys and the cane and said, "I'm Malcolm. You're Homer? I looked for you yesterday to introduce myself but I couldn't find you. I'm the new activities coordinator."

"Nice to meet you, Malcolm. I was at my piano lesson yesterday."

"Piano lesson? That's cool."

"Yeah. Gotta keep busy since I can't go out on the road anymore." They started walking down the hall.

"Oh, you used to travel?"

"I used to be a carny 'til this goddamn disease took that away from me."

"I'm sorry to hear that." Now Malcolm understood. The man wasn't drunk. He probably had Parkinson's.

Homer sighed. "I used to be an electrician a long time ago. Then I had to give that up when I couldn't do the work anymore and started the carny life. Loved it. Went all across the country for several years and wound up subbing for a guy at the Santa Monica Pier and decided if I had to retire, this was the place to be."

They got to the staircase, but Malcolm continued on down the hall to the elevator. Instead Homer started down the stairs. "You're okay going down the stairs?" Malcolm asked as he followed him down.

"I need to keep doing as much as I can. I can't let this thing beat me!"

"That's a good attitude." Malcolm pondered how he managed to play the piano with these shaking hands but decided that would be another conversation. "By the way, do you know what apartment George is in?"

"Second floor, too. You were right near it when I saw you."

"Oh, is it next door to Nick's?"

"Yep. That's the one." Homer shook his head. "Whoever put those two next to each other should have their head examined."

"You mean they don't get along?"

Homer threw his head back and laughed loudly. "That's an understatement! Those two make Hatfield and McCoy look like lovebirds!"

"The fight they had last night is nothing new?"

"What would be new is a night when they didn't have a fight." They had reached the community room, and Homer made a beeline to the piano and sat down. "Time to practice."

Malcolm watched him as he placed his trembling hands on the keys, curious to see how in the world Homer managed to play them. When those shaking fingers reached their destination and pressed down, the sound was undeniable. It was music. Maybe not like a concert pianist, but Homer played and his hands did not shake. "That's really good," Malcolm smiled at him.

"I ain't no Ray Charles, but it works."

"So piano playing stops the tremors?"

"Yep."

Malcolm stayed and listened until he noticed George had walked in with a newspaper and a cup of coffee. Malcolm joined him on the sofa. "Hey George, I wanted to see how you were doing after your fight with Nick last night."

George waved his hand dismissively. "No contest. He's a wuss."

Malcolm smiled. These two were quite the pair. "When's the game on today?"

"Not until 1. I've got a C-note on the Dodgers, but they haven't got a leg to stand on."

"Aren't they in first place?"

"Yeah but they've got too many on the injured list."

"Who are they playing?"

"The Cardinals, those bums. It's the only team that Kershaw can't dominate."

They watched in silence for a few minutes and then Malcolm decided to ask what he'd wanted to all along. "So what's the problem between you and Nick?"

"That wop?" He pretended to spit. "Lowest of the low."

"Did something specific happen between you two?"

"Ask him. His kind and my kind . . . they give me a lot of grief."

Malcolm was confused because he wasn't sure what George was referring to. He didn't know where either of them had come from. There was a touch of Irish brogue in George's voice. He hadn't heard Nick say more than a couple of grunts and grumbles so he had no way of placing an accent on him. They both had sounded like east coasters, but that was true of so many people in Los Angeles, and Malcolm was hardly an expert. "But I'm asking you. What are you referring to? What kind are you?"

George stared hard at Malcolm without saying a word. Malcolm wasn't sure why. Was he angry with him for asking? Did he expect Malcolm to know what he was talking about? Did he just think it was none of Malcolm's business? "Ask him," George finally said and turned his attention back to the television.

Malcolm took that as a signal to leave him alone and went back to the piano to listen to Homer's somewhat elementary rendition of "Sweet Home Chicago." Violet danced over to the piano and took Malcolm's arms. She twirled him around a couple of times and did a couple of soft-shoe steps. "Do you know how to tap dance, Malcolm?" she asked, fluttering her eyelashes.

"Can't say that I do."

"Oh you young people just dance wildly like your knickers are in a knot and you have to pee! Follow me." She proceeded to show Malcolm some line dance steps and he followed along. "Well bless your pea-pickin' heart! That's the ticket!"

Malcolm not only learned quickly, but also enjoyed himself immensely. He peeked at George to see if he had any interest, but George's eyes never left the screen. A couple of others in the room watched, however, and Malcolm danced over to them to see if they were interested in learning. They waved him off, but Malcolm's wheels were turning. This might be something. Have some of these older people teach what they know how to do. After Homer finished bemoaning his move to the land of California from his sweet home in Chicago, Malcolm thanked Violet for the lesson and went to the reception desk to get some paper and pencil. He wanted to make more lists about the folks who peopled the halls of this residence. He would find out what talents they had, where they were from, and made some notations on personality types and frailties. Not everyone was as spry or energetic as Violet.

62

9

MALCOLM GLANCED AT THE CLOCK WHEN HIS STOMACH GROWLED. He expected it to be about noon or one. Instead he was shocked to find out that it was almost three. He had been so absorbed in creating his list and defining his job that he lost track of time. There was no point in going out to lunch, since he was leaving to go home in an hour anyway. It had been quiet in the community room, just a few people coming and going. He hadn't seen any sign of Savali and had completely given up on ever seeing or hearing from the so-called activities director. Annabel would probably check in with him occasionally, but he didn't expect to see much of her either. Now that his chart was made, he had to interview everyone who lived there. That would be no small feat.

Savali appeared in front of him, dressed in her usual unisex outfit, but wearing hot red lipstick and smoky eye shadow. "Hey, are you hiding out or something?" she asked.

"I could ask you the same thing," Malcolm answered.

"I saw you in here but I didn't want to disturb you. You seemed so intent on what you were doing. So what are you doing?"

Malcolm shared his idea with Savali and although she wasn't quite as enthusiastic as he was, she agreed it might work at getting this group of people to be more inclusive. "Have you asked any of them yet?"

"No, but I figured Violet could teach line dancing to start. And maybe Homer could teach piano?"

"I doubt Homer could teach piano."

"Well, I know he's just learning himself, but he's better than someone who can't play at all."

"No, Malcolm. That's not what I meant. It would be more than he could handle. He's really been going downhill fast lately."

"You mean his Parkinson's?"

"Yeah. A month ago he was walking pretty well but now he can barely hold a fork to eat his dinner. Most of the time he gets hamburgers and pizza so he doesn't have to use a fork."

"Wow. I hadn't thought about all that. And it's all happened recently?"

"Yeah. Pretty much."

Malcolm was surprised that Savali knew so much about the residents. He didn't think she paid that much attention to them. "Maybe you can help me fill some of this out before I start walking the halls. You seem to know everyone."

"Let me look." Savali sat down and took the chart and then asked for his pen. She went through the list, jotting some things down while Malcolm watched. She handed him the list, stood abruptly and said, "It's a start." He watched her walk away or rather swish away. She could switch her mannerisms between masculine and feminine at her slightest whim.

After this display, Malcolm glanced down at the chart and was surprised to see how much of it Savali had filled out. She had cut his workload in half. The harder part was still ahead, however, convincing this group of old cranks that they had something both to offer and to accept from each other. "So Nick and George both know how to box. No wonder they were in competition with each other and in constant altercations," Malcolm muttered.

He saw that Violet could teach any kind of dancing, not just line. There were artists and craftspeople, able to teach everything from oils, charcoal and watercolors to quilting and needlepoint. There were writers and poets on the one hand, and electricians and plumbers on the other. Malcolm wasn't too sure there would be a great deal of interest in learning how to install a toilet or wire a lamp, but you never know. Actually, he had hoped for something less mundane and more offbeat, but then those would be the kinds of things that Savali probably wouldn't know about. They were those hidden talents that interesting eccentrics didn't shout out to the world.

It was time to go home and get ready for his next job. He hadn't done much today, but he felt tired and wondered how easy it was going to be to have two jobs. He hadn't thought this daytime one would be particularly taxing; certainly it didn't take anywhere near the energy and intensity of his restaurant job. But it did take a lot of mental stamina to deal with this idiosyncratic group of people.

He waved at Savali as he left and she winked back at him. "Maybe I'll see you later," she called out to him. He turned around and started to answer, but decided against it. He didn't really like her coming to the cafe with her boyfriends or whatever they were.

He walked quickly down the boardwalk and up Rose Avenue. It took longer than he thought to walk home, shower and dress, and get to work on time. Maybe he would have to change his hours and leave a little earlier. Or maybe he should wait and see whether this new job was going to pan out. He may do it just long enough to buy a car. And then who knows what might happen or where he might go.

His phone rang as he walked. The number was unfamiliar. He usually let it go to voice mail if he didn't recognize a number, but he thought it might be Annabel or that elusive activities director. "Hello?"

"Malcolm?"

"Yes, this is Malcolm."

"My name is John Siegel. I'm producing a film and I'm in a bind. One of my cameramen was taken to the hospital. Leslie Woods at CBS gave me your name. She had nothing but great things to say about you."

"Um, this would be a paying position?"

John laughed. "Of course."

"I mean it's not an internship or something?"

"No, Malcolm. This is the real thing. But I'd need you to start right away."

Malcolm didn't answer immediately. He felt this was an opportunity that he shouldn't pass up, but he knew he would have to quit both his jobs to be available at all times. He really wasn't excited by the prospect at all. How strange that the entertainment industry had suddenly lost its allure.

"Malcolm? Are you still there?"

"Uh, yeah. I guess I'm just surprised."

"Well I need an answer."

"Um, yeah, I think so."

"You think so?" John was truly taken aback. "Do you understand what I'm offering you? This is the big time. The film has backing and distributors."

"I'm sorry. I just started a new job that I'll now have to quit."

"I'm sure they'll understand when you tell them what it's for. So that's a yes?"

"Yes. When do I start and where do I go?"

"Tomorrow morning at nine. My office is in Studio City at CBS." He hung up abruptly.

What had he done? In a three-minute conversation his entire life had changed. He had to quit both his jobs and he had no idea when he would get paid, although it would be a nice chunk of change. But it meant he might have no income for months. And he had no car to get to the set and he had no idea where that might be.

He got home and got ready in a daze. He now had to tell his manager that he was quitting tonight! He wouldn't be giving them any notice and he was the one they had always counted on when people were irresponsible and didn't show up for work. And now he was giving them no notice and putting everyone else in a bind. And who was going to take his shifts?

He wasn't as worried about the new job. They could easily live without him. And no one was going to miss him, except maybe Savali. But probably not, since they had had little to do with each other for the last two days. But he knew deep down, that he was going to miss her.

10

OF COURSE MALCOLM HAD TO HAVE ONE OF HIS BEST TIP NIGHTS EVER, JUST TO MAKE HIM QUESTION HIS DECISION EVEN MORE. There was some kind of art gallery reception that brought in a lot of artists and art aficionados. Most of them had once been servers themselves, so they were excellent tippers. Besides enjoying the wad of cash in his pocket, Malcolm was happy to be so busy that he didn't have time to dwell on what he was going to have to do at the end of the night. And he certainly didn't have time to feel anxiety about the phone call to Annabel in the morning. As far as Savali and the rest of the gang at the senior residence were concerned, he wouldn't have to face them.

There was a lot of whooping and hollering at the end of the night when the wait staff sat at a table counting out their cash. Malcolm finished quickly and looked for Terry, the manager, who was in the office counting the night's take. "Can I talk to you?" Malcolm asked from the doorway.

"Sure, come on in. What a night!" Terry said sinking back in his chair.

"Yeah."

"What can I do for you? Need to change a shift?"

"Actually . . ." Malcolm took a deep breath. "I got a job offer as a cameraman on a film."

"That's fantastic! So do you need to take fewer shifts? You already work more than anyone else."

"I need to quit, I'm afraid . . . like tonight. The producer wants me to start tomorrow. I'm really sorry."

"Hey Malcolm, this is the restaurant business. It's the way it works. I get it. Don't worry. We'll figure it out."

Now Malcolm felt even worse. He really liked this job and the people he worked with. "Thanks. I appreciate it."

"You know, you'll always have a job here, Malcolm. In case things don't work out, I mean."

Malcolm just nodded. He felt a little bit of a lump in his throat, although he didn't know if he was apprehensive, sad, guilty or afraid. He left the restaurant without saying a word to the other servers. He didn't like goodbyes.

When he got home he went to his bank's website. His savings account hadn't changed much from the last time he looked. He had enough for food and transportation to last him a few months, but there went his chance at buying a car until he got paid from this new job. Luckily the taxes and insurance on the house wouldn't be due for another six months.

He slept fitfully, if at all, and woke up groggy with a dull headache. Besides the typical anxiety one feels the first day of any job, he hadn't been behind a camera in more than a year. He was unsure of his ability to do the job at all. He hoped the old saying about riding a bike would hold true.

He made the phone call to Annabel early enough for it to go to voice mail. She might end up calling him back, but at least he could postpone the conversation until he got home after his first day. He held out for the possibility that the job wouldn't happen for some reason. Maybe he hadn't kept up with the newest technology and couldn't do the job. Maybe he couldn't get to the set because of transportation problems. Or maybe the director and producers just wouldn't like him.

Taking buses in Los Angeles is never easy or quick, but he left himself two hours to get there and although it was rush hour, he was going against traffic. He walked in the doors of John's office exactly at nine. He didn't see how he was going to do this every day if it would take four hours coming and going. Maybe they'd give him an advance and he could buy a car. Well, at least he had been able to sleep some on the buses and he didn't feel quite as tired.

John greeted him and brought him inside his office. "Sit down Malcolm and sign these papers. We'll have to get going to the set, so I'll tell you about the film on the way. They're waiting for us so we have to hurry."

Malcolm signed the papers and followed John out the door. He knew he should have read what he was signing, but he felt rushed and intimidated. He got in the passenger seat of John's pick-up and they sped off, taking Ventura Boulevard to the 405 and then getting onto the Santa Monica Freeway toward the ocean, the exact place Malcolm had left two hours ago. "Where's the set?" Malcolm asked the silent John who had not said a word about the job or the movie since they left.

"Santa Monica."

Malcolm could have walked there from his house in about half an hour. "Is that where we'll be shooting the film?"

"Various places around town but we'll meet here every morning and then drive together."

"I live in Venice. Could I meet you at the set?"

"I suppose," John answered, obviously distracted.

Well, he may be a bit peeved about his morning of needless commuting, but at least he could cross one thing off his list of reasons for not doing this gig. John continued his silence and Malcolm decided it was best to leave John alone. He'd find out soon enough what the film was about and his place in it.

When they got to the Santa Monica studio, John rushed out of the car leaving Malcolm to stand by the side of the car, bewildered about where to go. He figured following John was probably the best approach, although he felt kind of silly watching everyone else hurrying around purposefully. John, however, seemed to have forgotten Malcolm was there, so he found one of the crewmembers at the coffee/bagel/donut table. "Hey man, I'm the new cameraman. John just hired me yesterday. I guess someone got sick or something?"

"Oh yeah. How ya doin'." The man continued stuffing his face and was absolutely no help in clueing Malcolm in on anything.

He was getting tired of starting jobs with no clear idea of what he was supposed to be doing. Well, in this one he knew what the job entailed, at least. He continued to try to get some information out of this man who was much more interested in eating and drinking the free food than sharing any knowledge about the film. "Can you point me to the director of photography?"

"Who? Oh, you mean Dan?"

"I don't know his name. I'm just trying to get an idea of what camera I'm operating or if I'm just an assistant."

"The guy who got sick was an operator."

"Okay. Well is Dan around?"

"Haven't seen him. Ask her." He pointed to a young woman with a clipboard rushing around the set, barking orders at people.

Malcolm caught up with the woman as she darted around the room. "Excuse me. I'm the replacement for the camera operator who got sick."

"Oh yes. Malcolm, right?"

"That's me."

"Ask Adam to show you the ropes. He's the other cameraman. He's the guy over there at the caterer's table." She pointed to the man Malcolm had just finished talking to. This set was as much of a zoo as the senior residence with no one being particularly helpful or instructive.

"Okay, thanks." He smiled and shook his head as he watched her scurry off. He went back to the coffee table and decided he might as well grab something to eat. Who knew when or whether there would be lunch in this madhouse. "She told me to talk to you." Malcolm grabbed a bagel and coffee. "I'm Malcolm and I believe she said your name is Adam?"

"Yeah. Nice to meet you." Adam took another donut as he walked away. "This way. It's you and me and two assistants."

Malcolm followed him and bit his tongue. He really wanted to ask him why he had told him to go elsewhere, but since he'd be working with him, he thought it best not to. "I don't even know what the film is about. I haven't seen the script."

"It'll be a breeze. No hard shots . . . very straightforward. Just you and me on either side of them."

"Who do you mean by them?"

"Mandy and Blake. It's not rocket science. Doing it on the beach, doing it in the car, doing it on the desk."

"You mean this is a porn movie?"

Adam stared at him. "Duh. What did you think with a name like "Sleeping with Seattle?"

Malcolm stared back at him. "I---I didn't know the name," he finally said.

"Hey, it's a job."

"I guess you could call it that." Crap. What had he done? He quit two jobs he liked; well the jury's still out on the activities coordinator one, but it certainly was better than this by a long shot. He didn't want to do this at all. He would be embarrassed professionally and he didn't want this on his resume. Could he walk out? He hadn't even read the contract he signed; everything had been done so hastily this morning. He doubted they'd actually come after him if he walked out, but would this damage his camera operating career in the future, if there actually was a career in the future.

"Hello? You listening?"

Malcolm realized that Adam had been talking to him. He also realized that he wasn't going to do this. "Sorry, man. I'm not interested."

"Hey, we start shooting today. Where are you going?"

Malcolm just waved his arm and went off to find John. So that's why he wouldn't tell him anything in the car. Malcolm started to seethe. Yeah right. John had made it all sound legitimate. The big time – ha! By the time he found John, his anger had been building and he felt no remorse or embarrassment at quitting. In fact, he felt emboldened. "John, you didn't tell me this was a porn film."

"Yeah, so?"

"So I'm not interested."

"You signed a contract, Malcolm."

"Go ahead and sue me." And at that Malcolm stomped off. He took out his phone and dialed Annabel's number first. It went to voicemail, but that didn't deter him. "Annabel? It's Malcolm. Disregard my first message. I'll be at work by noon. And I'm really sorry." He hung up and dialed the restaurant. He spoke to the day manager and told her to please leave a message for the night manager that he was rescinding his resignation and to call him. He breathed a sigh of relief as he hung up and sprinted toward the beach and boardwalk.

11

MALCOLM HUGGED SAVALI WHEN HE SAW HER STANDING IN THE LOBBY. It was a spontaneous gesture and he jerked back when he realized what he had done. She was as surprised as he was. "Well, that was nice but what was it for?" she asked. "And Annabel told me you quit, so what are you doing here anyway?"

"I did but now I'm back. Just forget it. A momentary lapse in judgment."

"What are you talking about? Are you crazy? Never mind. Yeah, you are."

"I'll tell you the story some time. Right now I just want to do whatever it is I do here."

"Welcome back." She winked at him and went into the back office.

Malcolm found the community room empty. The television wasn't on. No one played cards. Even Violet wasn't looking for her latest conquest. That was weird. He went down the hall and found one of the residents coming out of his room. "I thought you quit," the man said. "That's what George said."

"I did. But it was a mistake. I'm back. Where is George? He's not watching the game on television."

"No game today. And it's Tuesday. He goes to the gym."

"Oh yeah? I didn't know he went to the gym."

"Tuesdays and Thursdays."

"That's good. He keeps in shape."

"He was a boxer, you know."

"I heard that. How about you, Joseph? What do you like to do?"

Joseph shrugged. "Play the ponies. That takes up most of my time."

"Do you win?"

"Once in a while. Don't want to win too much. It'll only go to the IRS."

"Huh?" Malcolm asked.

"I owe them money. My lawyer worked out a deal that they would be the beneficiaries of my estate. My goal in life, now, is to spend it all before I croak."

"Well, you probably picked a good way to lose it all. From what I understand, the odds of winning at the track are pretty slim."

Joseph grinned. "Ain't that the truth!" He walked down the hall and Malcolm continued up to Nick's room. He had developed some kind of fascination with Nick and his cantankerousness and he wanted to know more about his past. Maybe it's because he was the least likely to share it of the whole group. Everything he knew about him he had gotten from Savali and George.

He knocked on Nick's door. "Go away!" Nick yelled.

He wanted to say that it was Malcolm, but he wasn't sure if that would make Nick open the door or tell him to scram with even more forcefulness. He stayed silent but knocked again . . . and again. Finally Nick answered the door. "Hey, Nick," Malcolm smiled at him.

"What the hell do you want? I'm busy. Anyway, I thought you were outta here."

"I'm back. I wanted to talk to you about your boxing. Were you a professional?"

Nick stared hard at him, almost looking through him. "What the hell are you talking about and why the fuck do you care?"

"I . . . um . . . am trying to find out what talents people have that they could teach to others. I thought we could start some classes for the residents."

"You've got to be kidding."

"No. I'm not kidding."

Nick shook his head. "You think the people here want to go to school? You think they're interested in spending time with each other? You think they give a shit about anything?" He shook his head again. "You better go back to the drawing board." He started to close the door but Malcolm stuck his foot in it.

"I'd like to hear more about what ideas you might have, then."

"Ideas about what?"

"Activities you'd like to see here."

"Activities for what? I don't want any activities. Now will you just leave me alone? I said I was busy." He tried to close the door again, but this time Malcolm just followed him inside. "Jesus Christ! What's the matter with you? You don't hear me? I said leave me alone."

Malcolm noticed a huge pile of papers and notebooks in one corner of the room. He noticed a newer Mac laptop open on a table and an ashtray next to it, filled to the brim with cigar butts. Other than the table with two chairs, a dresser and a bed, the room was pretty barren. Nothing was on the walls except a couple of shelves that were filled with books. Malcolm went over and took a book off a shelf. "Edgar Allen Poe's poems." He looked at a couple of others. "Walt Whitman, Robert Frost, Yeats, Wordsworth, Langston Hughes. I see you like American poets." Malcolm glanced at the screen of the laptop. "You write poetry?"

"Yeah. So?"

"That's cool. Never would have thought you were a poet."

"Well I'm not interested in teaching it to any of these losers."

"How about boxing? Would you teach that?"

"You really are deaf."

"No. Just persistent."

"Stubborn."

"Can I read some of your poems?"

"For what?"

"I'm curious. Do you mind?"

Nick shrugged his shoulders and Malcolm took that as a yes. He went to the pile of papers and notebooks and took a notebook off and opened it. It was a poem titled "Angels in the Gutter." Malcolm sat at the table and read. He spent several minutes reading through the notebook. Nick, meanwhile, paced back and forth. He was obviously uncomfortable. "Okay, that's enough. I want to get back to work."

Malcolm looked incredulously up at Nick. "Wow. These are really good."

"You don't have to be so surprised."

"Well, it just doesn't fit your persona, I guess."

"Why not? What the hell do you know about my persona?"

"I guess your New Jersey accent and boxing background."

"What? You had me pegged as a mobster?"

"Sort of."

Nick nodded. "And mobsters can't write poetry?"

"I guess I didn't think they were into that kind of thing."

Nick let out a loud belly laugh and that really caught Malcolm even more off guard. He had never seen Nick smile, no less laugh. "You are something else, Malcolm!"

Malcolm wasn't sure what Nick was laughing at exactly. That he thought he was a mobster? That he couldn't believe he was a poet? Both? "What's funny, Nick?"

"You."

Malcolm decided at this point to leave it alone. He thought this would be a good time to depart, with Nick smiling. "Thanks for letting me read your poems. I'd like to read more of them." Nick waved him off, but Malcolm decided that he would also take that as a yes.

Malcolm spent the rest of the afternoon chatting with the residents and garnering ideas for his classes. Other than a handful of the more curmudgeonly ones like Nick and George, they were eager to teach each other. Annabel stopped in, happy to see him and happy that he was actually going to do something to earn his salary. She liked his idea so much that she said she'd be sharing it with the Activities Director to set up at the other sites.

Even Savali got into it. "Let's see what you got," she said as she joined him at a table in the community room. She took the paper he'd been working on. "Nick's gonna teach poetry and boxing? Ha! Good luck with that!"

"I read his poems. They're really good. Did you know he wrote poetry?"

"Nope. Next you're gonna tell me that George is a ballet dancer."

Malcolm smiled. "I haven't seen him to ask. Maybe he's got something up his sleeve too."

"How about you, Malcolm? What do you do that will blow me away?"

He smiled at her. "Nothing . . . no surprises here." He tilted his head and raised his eyebrows. "And you?" Maybe he would finally get an answer to his questions about her. Was she transgender? Was she male? Female? Was it all one big joke?

"Nope. No surprises here either." She grinned at him and left.

He tried not to let her teasing get to him, but it wasn't easy. It was not just that he wasn't able to find out the truth about her, but he couldn't stand the way she mocked him and was so provocative. And dammit, he was so attracted to her!

He left at four without saying goodbye to Savali. When he got to the cafe an hour later, he was greeted with hugs and high fives by all the servers and kitchen workers, as well as the manager. He was glad to be back. It felt good to be liked and cared about.

12

AFTER A FEW WEEKS MALCOLM AND THE RESIDENTS FELL INTO A ROUTINE. From ten to twelve every day, they met informally in the community room to teach and learn. Monday was Arts and Crafts Day: those who could draw, paint, sculpt, knit, or crochet taught anyone who was interested in learning. It was casual and unscripted, and mostly filled with women, although Malcolm tried hard to get the men to come. Tuesday was Music Day: Homer taught piano and Jose, the maintenance man, taught guitar. The students were a good coed mix. Wednesday was Physical Education: Violet taught dancing from ten to eleven and from eleven to twelve Savali taught yoga and Pilates and once again, it was mostly women. Malcolm had been trying to convince George and Nick to teach boxing, but he hadn't been successful. George wouldn't do it with Nick and Nick wouldn't do it with George. Thursday was a Writers Workshop where the same group of residents shared and critiqued each other's work. Again, Malcolm tried to convince Nick to come and do a poetry workshop but to no avail. Friday was Game Day. Malcolm had hoped to introduce a whole slew of different games, having read that keeping an active brain was important for the elderly. But it was basically the same card players that were always there, playing Gin Rummy, Poker and Pinochle.

So yes, things were going somewhat smoothly. People liked the activities, and Malcolm enjoyed the mornings, learning new things. In the afternoons he made himself available to work with the residents with their smartphones and computers. He also helped them with paperwork they had to fill out for various government agencies, insurance, taxes, travel etc. And he and Jose had set up a couple of afternoons a week when they helped the residents with tasks in their apartments that had become difficult for them to perform like setting up furniture or fixing small appliances. But it had also turned into a time where the two of them ended up cleaning some of the apartments for the residents.

Since Nick basically refused to partake of any of the activities, Malcolm had to make a concerted effort to see him by going to his apartment. And it was always the same silly dance: Nick would be grouchy about his coming and Malcolm would push himself into the apartment. Once inside, however, Nick softened a little and Malcolm even detected a little pleasure on Nick's part at having a visitor. They talked about poetry mostly, although Malcolm tried hard to get Nick to talk about his past. The other residents seemed eager to share their life stories, but not Nick. Malcolm decided to share his, hoping this would open Nick up, but so far, no cigar.

One Friday morning Malcolm was in the community room playing poker with George and a few others and Nick walked in. "Oh great, look what the cat dragged in," George sneered.

"Up yours, asshole," Nick answered back. "Malcolm, I need to talk to you."

Malcolm got up from the table. "Here guys, read 'em and weep." He put his hand down on the table.

"Ha! Weep over a pair of sixes?" George laughed.

Malcolm smiled and left with Nick. "Do you want to go back to your apartment to talk?" he asked.

"No. Let's take a walk," Nick said and took Malcolm's arm to lead him outside.

This was a strange turn of events, but Malcolm was actually thrilled. "Okay. Beach? Boardwalk?"

Nick didn't answer but walked over the boardwalk to the beach, so Malcolm just followed his lead. They walked south toward Marina del Rey and Malcolm just waited for Nick to start talking. But he didn't. After about five or ten minutes Malcolm opened his mouth. "So what's up?"

Nick looked around them furtively, checking to see if anyone was close enough to hear their conversation. "I got a problem."

"What's that?"

"I gotta get outta here."

"Here being your apartment? Venice? California?"

"All of the above."

"Why?"

"Can't tell you."

"Okay, but why are you telling me then?"

"I need help."

"What do you want me to do?"

Nick was quiet for a couple of minutes, breathing heavily. He finally spoke. "I need a ride and I need to borrow some money."

Malcolm stopped walking. Nick had not been looking at him while they spoke and Malcolm took Nick's arm and turned him to face him. "Why me? I hardly have extra money to lend you. I barely get by. And I don't even own a vehicle."

"I thought you'd have a car. And I don't really have anyone else to ask."

"I thought you'd lived here a long time. You don't know anyone here better than you know me?"

Nick shook his head. "Nope."

"I don't know what I can do. I mean I guess I could lend you a little money. How much do you need?"

"I'm not sure. Maybe a thousand?"

Malcolm's eyes widened. "A thousand? That's a lot."

"I need a plane ticket and it's not like I can wait fourteen days for the economy seat!" Nick's voice was getting louder and gruffer.

Malcolm exhaled loudly. "I'd like to help you, Nick, but I don't know how. Is there anything I can do besides give you money or a ride to the airport?"

Nick turned around abruptly. "No." He started walking back up the sand. He stopped and turned toward Malcolm. "But thanks."

Malcolm watched him walk away and then hurried after him. "Where do you need to go? Maybe I could rent a car and drive you there."

Nick shrugged. "Nowhere in particular. Just away from here."

They walked in silence for several minutes while Malcolm tried to make sense of it all. What was Nick running away from? Apparently he wasn't running toward anywhere specific. He was being awfully secretive and evasive, but Malcolm wanted to help. "If you just need a place to stay for a few days, you could crash at my house."

Nick stopped abruptly again and took Malcolm's arm. "I would really appreciate that."

Malcolm was a bit taken aback. He had made the offer figuring Nick would never take him up on it. Nick was not the kind of person to share living quarters or accept kindness. He must be scared and desperate. And Malcolm was convinced that there was something criminal and illegal about the whole thing. "Okay," Malcolm answered tentatively.

"Could we go now? I could give you the key to my apartment and you could bring me some things," Nick said.

"Well, I guess so." Malcolm's voice did not mask his consternation.

"Where do you live?"

"Off of Rose Avenue."

"Near the boardwalk?"

"No further up. Past Lincoln."

"Good. Let's go." Nick started walking again this time toward the street. "Let's go up Westminster."

"It's a bit longer. It's easier and quicker to go up the boardwalk."

"No. I'd prefer to stay away from the apartment area."

Malcolm shrugged. They walked all the way to the house in silence. Malcolm knew that asking Nick any questions would be fruitless and he also knew that Nick was probably not interested in talking at all. Malcolm hoped that he wasn't harboring a criminal, but he was pretty sure that it was probably the case. "I'd better let Savali know I'll be gone for awhile," he said as he dialed the office number.

"Savali doesn't give a shit."

"Maybe not, but I'd feel better letting her know."

"You're a good kid, Malcolm."

Malcolm had no idea how to respond to this totally uncharacteristic remark. Nick must be really frightened to resort to being nice. And then Malcolm realized that it was probably not meant as a complimentary comment, but a sarcastic put-down. "Here we are," he said as they approached his front door. He unlocked it and held it open for Nick.

"Nice place. You live alone in this big house?"

"Yes."

"What are you doing renting such a big place?"

"Actually I own it."

Nick narrowed his eyes suspiciously. "You own a house in Venice and you can't lend me a G note?"

"I inherited it."

"Lucky guy."

"If you want to look at it that way. I wouldn't say so."

Nick raised his eyebrows and shrugged. "Whatever. Anyway, thanks again." He reached in his pocket and handed Malcolm the key to his apartment. "There's a suitcase in the closet. Maybe just some clothes and toothbrush, razor, you know, things like that."

"How about your computer?"

"Oh yeah. Bring that."

"And your notebooks?"

"You gonna fit all that in a suitcase?"

"I'll try." Malcolm looked at the time on his phone. "I'd better get back. There's not a lot of food, but help yourself to anything."

Nick just nodded. Malcolm left and walked briskly as he pondered what in the world he had gotten himself into.

13

MALCOLM HURRIED BACK TO MOSS HOUSE. It was now almost time to head to the café and he still had plenty to do. He slipped into the residence and tried to duck from a possible interrogation from Savali. It wasn't like him to stay out for a few hours. In fact, he rarely took more than fifteen minutes for lunch, when he took it at all. Savali, on the other hand, could be gone for hours at a time. Depending on her mood or identity that day, she might be shopping or at Muscle Beach. He would also have to sneak out with Nick's suitcase because she would surely wonder what that was all about.

Malcolm was in luck. Savali was in the back office when he got there, talking on the phone. He got to Nick's apartment and opened the door. He found the suitcase in the closet and filled it first with what Malcolm felt was most important: Nick's poetry notebooks and computer. That didn't leave a lot of room for clothes, but those could be replaced or even borrowed from Malcolm, if necessary. He managed to squeeze in the essentials: underwear, a couple of shirts, a pair of pants and the basic toiletries.

Just as he zipped the suitcase closed, there was a knock at the door. "Nick?" Crap. It was Savali. Malcolm tried to think fast about what to say, but his mind was blank. "Nick, please open up. It's important." Malcolm still waited, hoping she'd go away. But she didn't. Rather she took out a passkey and opened the door. "Malcolm! Where's Nick?"

Malcolm saw a man standing behind Savali, who was not the spitting image of Nick, but sure looked like a family member. He was dressed in a shiny, expensive suit. His hair was slicked back and obviously dyed black. His face was tanned and it looked like he was wearing makeup. "He's not here," Malcolm answered, trying to sound definitive.

"Where is he? And why are you in his apartment?"

"He had asked me to fix something for him. Jose let me in," he lied. "Who's your friend?"

"This is Nick's brother, Anthony. He needs to speak to Nick."

"Well, he's not here."

"I can see that! What's with the suitcase?"

"Uh, it's broken. I'm just throwing it out. Nick asked me to. Anyway, do you make a habit out of entering people's apartments when they're not here?"

Savali glared at Malcolm. "No. I don't. But I use my discretion when I think it's important. Haven't you ever seen the commercial?"

"Oh, you mean 'I've fallen and I can't get up?'"

"Yeah. That one."

Malcolm took a deep breath. "Well, as you see, Nick's not here and I need to get to my other job," he said as he picked up the suitcase and brushed by her. "Nice meeting you, Anthony," he said in passing. He rushed down the stairs and finally put the suitcase down to roll when he got to the Speedway. Was Nick hiding from his brother? And then there was Savali. He doubted she would let up on him about what he was doing in Nick's apartment.

He got home with barely enough time to shower and leave for work. Nick was in the living room, watching television. Malcolm handed him the suitcase without telling him what had gone on. He didn't have time for a long conversation and he wanted to get the straight story once and for all, so he would wait until he got home. "I'll probably be home about eleven. Will you be up?" Malcolm asked Nick with his hand on the front door knob, ready to leave.

"How should I know? Why do you care?"

"I need to talk to you and I don't have time now."

"What do you need to talk about?" Nick asked, irritably.

"I just told you. I have to go to work."

"Work where?"

"I'm a waiter at Cafe Gratitude."

"Well, let's make a deal. I'll wait up for you if you bring me back some dinner."

Malcolm shook his head and smiled. "Fine, if that's what it takes."

"Well, your kitchen isn't exactly well stocked."

Malcolm couldn't argue that one. "Is there anything specific you want?"

"I'm not picky. Just don't make it too healthy."

"Right. Got it." Malcolm left, knowing he'd be stopping at the Mexican restaurant he would pass on his way home. He would never hear the end of it if he brought dinner home from Cafe Gratitude.

It was a busy night at the cafe, and since one of the servers called in sick at the last minute, Malcolm's net take home was close to three hundred dollars. He might be able to get that car sooner than he had originally thought.

Nick was asleep in front of the television when Malcolm entered the living room. He set the bag of Mexican food on the dining room table and called out, "Nick! Wake up! Your food is here."

Nick opened his eyes and grumbled, "Took you long enough."

Malcolm ignored him and opened the refrigerator. "Do you want a beer?"

"Yeah, and what did you bring me?"

"Burritos."

"I like tacos better."

"Life's tough." Malcolm got a couple of plates and set them and the beer down on the table. He opened the bag and put the food out on the plates, pulled up a chair, and had already taken a bite by the time Nick got to the table.

Nick sat down and ate with gusto. They finished their meal in silence, both of them apparently hungrier than they had realized.

"You got another beer?" Nick asked as he downed the last of the bottle in his hand.

Malcolm got two more beers from the refrigerator. "Your brother was looking for you. He came in with Savali when I was in your room."

Nick guzzled half his beer before answering. "Yeah, I know."

"Is that why you want to leave town?"

"Partly."

"That's kind of a heavy duty reaction to not wanting to see your brother. You could just tell him to go away."

"It's not that simple."

"You afraid he's going to hurt you or something? What the heck happened between you?"

"I don't want to talk about it."

"I think you need to. You're asking me for money but you won't tell me why? You think that's fair?"

"You can't give me any money anyway, so I don't owe you an explanation. I'll leave in the morning."

"You can stay here, Nick. But it's not just the money. You know Savali's going to ask me and your brother will probably be back.

What am I supposed to tell them? They found me in your apartment with a suitcase."

Nick sat back in his chair and finished his beer. "Well then, maybe I shouldn't stay here and put you in this situation."

"I'm already in this situation, whether you stay here or not. So you might as well stay until we figure something out."

"You got a toothpick?"

Malcolm got him a toothpick and sat back down. "Does this involve criminal activity?"

Nick picked at his teeth for a couple of minutes. "Okay. I guess you ought to know what's going on." He opened the bag and dropped his toothpick into the wad of greasy wrappers. "My family is into drug trafficking. I was part of the business until a year ago when I left and moved here. I changed my name and thought I was safe until my brother called yesterday and sweet-talked Savali into verifying that I lived there."

"Are you in witness protection?"

"No. Nothing like that."

"Why'd you leave?"

"My son told me he'd never have anything to do with me if I didn't."

"Who else in your family besides your brother is in it?"

"My mother and father and all their relatives."

"Your mother and father are still alive?"

"Yeah."

"They're still in the business?"

"Yep."

"They've never been caught?"

"They managed to get out of it whenever they were arrested. All it takes is money, you know. Anybody can be bought."

"Then why don't you have any money?"

"I left it all behind. I had a boat, fancy cars, big beautiful house." Nick looked down at his mismatched shirt and pants. "And now look at me. I shop at thrift stores.

"Where's your son, then? He's the one who asked you to leave."

"He's in San Diego. He lives with his mother. He's a good kid and never got involved in the business."

"How old is he?"

"Probably about your age. I haven't seen him in a while."

"But you saw him a year ago, right? When he asked you to get out of the business?"

"Nah, I didn't see him. I just sent them money every month. I didn't want them to know anything in case they were ever asked. He didn't know until recently where his child support came from. Someday I hope to see him again. I just wanted enough time to pass, so no one would be looking for me. And now my brother comes along."

"So you left without telling any member of your family where you were?"

"That's right."

"Where do they live?"

"San Francisco."

"How do you think your brother found you?"

Nick just shook his head. "No idea."

"Why would he look for you? I mean if you're out of the business, what difference does it make to him?"

"He's afraid I'll tell someone and out them all."

"Why would you do that?"

"I wouldn't. But he doesn't know that. Once you get involved in the crime business, you don't trust anyone."

"So what would he do if you saw him?"

"Probably kill me with regards from the boss."

Malcolm sat back in his chair and exhaled deeply. "Well, that sucks."

"That would be an understatement." Nick stood. "Well, I'm going to bed. I found the room with a bed in it that looks like it isn't yours. Shall I sleep there?"

"Sure." Malcolm started thinking of everything a roommate might need. "Hey, do you need some money to buy yourself some groceries?"

"I don't think I should go outside. I'll manage with the crap you have in your cupboards and fridge."

"I'll get some stuff tomorrow. What do you want?"

"Doesn't matter. I won't be here long." Nick left and Malcolm sat back in his chair for quite a while, thinking of the mess he had gotten into.

14

MALCOLM WOKE UP EARLY THE NEXT MORNING, ASSUMING NICK WAS STILL ASLEEP. Yet, he found Nick at the dining room table, typing on his laptop. "Oh. Good morning."

Nick looked up. "Did you think I would have run out in the middle of the night? You seem surprised to see me."

"No. I just thought you were still in bed."

"Well, I'm not."

"Yes. I see that. Do you want some cereal?" he called from the kitchen.

"Sure."

"Are you writing poetry?" Malcolm asked, setting the bowls on the table.

Nick stopped typing and grinned at Malcolm. "You act like you're my mother. You have nothing better to do than worry about what I'm doing?"

"Sorry. Don't mean to pry." He started to shovel the cereal into his mouth.

"You just don't act like a normal twenty-something kid." Nick stared at the bowlful before him. "You trying to make me fat?"

"What?"

"This is a lot of cereal for a guy my age. I'm not a growing boy like you." Malcolm shrugged and continued shoveling his cereal. He was anxious to get out of there, although also apprehensive about going to work. He was not looking forward to the grilling he was going to get from Savali. "Actually, I was looking at plane tickets. Jesus, they're expensive!"

"Where were you looking to go?"

"I was looking at someplace like Alabama where there's little activity from families like ours. No one would recognize me."

"I don't think you'd like living in Alabama."

Nick grinned again. "Like that matters. It's not like I'm living the life of Riley in Venice. I just want to stay alive so I can see my son again."

"How do you live? I mean, financially?"

"Social Security."

"How'd you manage that?"

"I set it up before I left. I gave the Feds some information. I'm not formally in Witness Protection, but there are other ways they help."

"So I assume Nick Bailey isn't your real name?"

"That's correct."

Malcolm stood up and put his bowl in the sink. "I'm going to be late if I don't get going," he called over his shoulder. "See you later. I'm not working tonight so I'll stop at the grocery store on my way home." Nick didn't answer.

Malcolm tried to craft his answers to Savali, as he walked. He hoped Anthony wasn't there. Malcolm had to admit to feeling a little frightened of him. But then, he should probably also feel a little frightened of Nick, now that he knew the truth about him. These weren't a couple of two-bit criminals. This was the Mafia or something similar. Did Nick have a gun on him? Could Malcolm be arrested for aiding and abetting? By the time he got to work, he had worked himself into a major case of paranoia.

"Well, well, well. If it isn't Mr. Secret Agent Man." Savali looked up from her computer when Malcolm walked in.

Malcolm stiffened. "Secret Agent Man?"

"You never heard of the song?"

Malcolm breathed a sigh of relief. She was just being her usual sardonic self. "Yeah, I've heard of it."

"So you know where Nick is, but you're not telling?"

"What can you tell me about his brother?"

"Let's see." Savali said smugly. "His name is Anthony Balducci and he lives in San Francisco. Anything else you want to know about him? Oh, and apparently Nick's name is really Dominick Balducci, not Nick Bailey."

"Uh huh. And why is Anthony here?"

Savali's red lips drew thin. "I believe it's your turn to answer."

"Answer what?"

"Where's Nick?"

"Isn't he here?"

"No," Savali answered dryly. "So, do you want to know why Anthony's here looking for Nick or not?"

"Not really. I need to get to work." At that Malcolm went into the community room to set it up for the day's activity. Today was Thursday: Writer's Workshop. All he had to do was push a few tables together. But he wished there was more to do to avoid Savali asking more questions. He didn't even have any writing to pretend to be poring over. Malcolm sat in, but so far he hadn't brought any writing.

Malcolm had always wanted to write. He felt like he'd had an intriguing past that could be good fodder for a novel. Actually, Nick's story might be the most lucrative one to write, if only he could get it out of him.

The members of the workshop started trickling in. The group was a good cross-section of the residents. And it was growing. At first only those that had written journals or stories most of their lives showed up. But lately, as word spread, people who had never written before started coming with work that was in need of a great deal of editing. But the more experienced writers were helpful in their critiquing. That gave Malcolm more impetus to finally get some words down on paper and join the group as a full-fledged member. Maybe he'd write tonight since he didn't have to work at the restaurant.

Anthony did show up again and made a beeline for Malcolm, knowing that he was the key to finding Nick. "Hey, I must speak to my brother. It's really important."

Malcolm shushed him. At the end of the workshop, everyone wrote silently to a prompt and then read it aloud. This was not to be critiqued, just a short quick-write that was fun to end the morning. Malcolm did join them for the quick-write and pushed a piece of paper and pen over to Anthony so he, too, could participate. But he shook his head and sat back in his chair, perfectly willing to wait for Malcolm to finish. Every time Malcolm glanced over, he saw Anthony staring at him with arms crossed and his mouth in a perpetual smirk.

When everyone finished reading their prompts and got up from the table, Malcolm bought a little time by having to break apart the tables. "Anthony, I have a lot of work to do."

"Just tell me where I can find him. I have to speak to him."

"Why do you need to talk to him?" Malcolm asked.

"It's personal stuff."

"I can't help you."

"I don't think you understand. This is a matter of life and death."

Malcolm called his bluff. "Whose?"

Anthony gritted his teeth. "Tell my brother that his mother is dying and he ought to come see her. She asked for him."

"This is the family business you're talking about?" Malcolm's voice was stronger than his resolve.

"Just tell him he needs to go home. I wanted to bring him with me. You know, so he could fly back in style. But I don't have time for this. You tell him he needs to come home." Anthony started to leave and then turned abruptly. "And you better tell him." He finally left.

Malcolm felt a knot in his stomach grow tighter. *I better tell him or what?* He hurried off to find a new distraction.

A bulletin board had been set up where people could post things they needed help with. Everyday there were computer or smartphone problems that needed to be resolved and household tasks that needed to get accomplished. The board was usually full and that was how Malcolm's afternoons were spent. And none of these tasks took less than an hour because it had to include a lot of conversation.

Savali left Malcolm alone for the rest of the day. He wasn't sure if she was avoiding him or she was just busy, but he was glad that her interrogation had ended for now. He snuck out at four without saying goodbye to her.

He stopped at Whole Foods on the way home and bought groceries and take-out. Nick seemed genuinely happy to see him when he walked inside, probably only because he was hungry. "What'd ya bring for dinner?"

Malcolm was right. "A bunch of different things." He set the containers on the dining room table and went into the kitchen to put the groceries away.

"You didn't pack any forks!" Nick yelled from the table.

"Just a minute," Malcolm grumbled. He came in with plates, forks, knives, and napkins.

"Why didn't you just bring some plastic stuff from the store? That way you wouldn't have to wash any dishes."

"That's a waste of resources."

"Well excuse me, Mother Nature!"

Malcolm glared at him but said nothing. He waited a couple of minutes so the food would make Nick a little less grumpy before bringing up the subject of his brother. "Anthony was there again today. This time he was a little more aggressive. And Savali's giving me the third degree, too, trying to find out whether I know where you are.

Nick put his fork down and glanced sheepishly at Malcolm. "I'm sorry I got you into this. I really am. I'll leave after dinner."

"No, Nick," Malcolm sighed. "That's not what I mean. You don't have to leave. I just wanted to tell you that your brother is going to be relentless in pursuing you."

"Yeah, well, that's the way he is."

"Do you know why he's looking for you? I mean for sure? Or are you just guessing?"

"What are you getting at, Malcolm? Spit it out."

"Anthony said your mother is dying and she asked for you."

Nick was silent. He sat back in his chair, folded his arms, and scowled. "He's probably full of shit."

"Maybe he's not. Is there some way you could find out? Like call?"

"No. I don't want to."

"But if it's true, and she's dying and asked for you, could you live with yourself if you don't at least call her?"

"Stop being so dramatic, Malcolm."

Nick went back to eating and Malcolm eventually joined him. They ate in silence for the rest of dinner, politely passing containers of food back and forth. After dinner, Nick went back to his computer and Malcolm went to his room. It was not the way Malcolm had hoped to spend his night off.

15

THE NEXT MORNING, NICK WAS ALREADY IN THE KITCHEN WITH A CUP OF COFFEE IN HAND, WHEN MALCOLM ENTERED. "You're up early," Malcolm said as he poured himself a cup.

"Well, you finally bought some decent coffee so there was a reason to get up."

"I'm working day and night today. I'll only be home to shower and change clothes and probably I'll be late getting home tonight since it's Friday. You'll have to figure out your own meals."

"I'll be fine. Don't worry about it." Nick cleared his throat. "I did some research last night on the computer."

Malcolm waited for Nick to continue, but finally asked. "Oh yeah? About what?"

"My mother actually is in the hospital."

"So your brother wasn't lying about that?"

"Apparently not."

"Where?"

"San Francisco."

"What are you going to do?"

"Nothing. There's nothing I can do. She's old. She's dying. That's what old people do."

"Sometimes it's young people who die." Malcolm was thinking of his own mother.

"Well, my mother's old."

"Would you want to see her if you could?"

"Don't you have to go to work?"

Malcolm wouldn't let it go. "Maybe we can figure out a way to get you money for a plane ticket."

"And then what? If I visited her, my brother would find me."

Malcolm smiled. "Maybe we could disguise you?"

"Oh for God's sake, Malcolm. Don't be an idiot!"

"Okay, dumb idea. But Anthony wouldn't come after you at your mother's bedside."

"No, but he'd get me outside the hospital."

"Not if your mother told him not to. Isn't that true? And if your mother really did ask for you . . ."

Nick didn't answer right away, but Malcolm knew he had touched a nerve. Malcolm put his cup in the sink and started to leave. "Maybe I'll see what a plane ticket costs," Nick finally muttered.

On his walk to work, Malcolm filled his head with thinking of ways Nick could make money. By the time he got to work, he had worked himself up into a frenzy of sorts. He started by worrying about Nick, but wound up fretting about the direction his own life was taking.

"Hey Secret Agent Man," Savali called out to him as he walked past the reception desk.

"The name is Bond, James Bond." Malcolm winked at her as he walked past her into the community room. It was Game Day. He had to get the tables and chairs ready. Homer was in there, practicing on the piano. It was quite a sight to behold. Homer's hands would be shaking uncontrollably until he got them positioned on the keys, not always an easy task. But once he was able to press his fingers down, the transformation was instantaneous and remarkable. Notes were played with precision and strength. The songs were simple, but musical and enjoyable. Malcolm never tired of watching this process.

Homer had to focus on his playing and hadn't noticed Malcolm for several minutes. When he finally did, he shouted out to him, "Malcolm, my man!"

"Hey, Homer. You've expanded your repertoire."

"Yup. I got 'I've Been Working on the Railroad' down pat. You know this one?" Malcolm shrugged, feeling badly that he didn't. "How about 'Down in the Valley'?"

"I didn't have much chance as a kid to learn these songs."

"That's a shame. Do you know 'Oh Susanna'?" Homer started to play and Malcolm nodded.

He started to sing along when George walked in. "What's on tap for today's games?" he asked.

"Do you have a suggestion? We are trying to move into some alternatives to the usual card and board games."

"Asking the wrong person. I don't like change much."

"It's never too late to start."

Homer agreed. "Look at me. I just started the piano a year ago."

George laughed. "Ah, forget it. I'm not interested. I'll stick to the games I can win at." Malcolm shook his head and smirked while Homer went back to playing his song.

Some of the others trickled in and soon the tables were full and the cards were dealt. Other than one table of Jewish and Chinese women playing Mahjongg, it was mostly groups of men playing cards: gin rummy, poker, or pinochle, depending on their ethnicity and what part of the country the men were from. Malcolm had not done any scientific survey, but it seemed to him that the New York Jews played pinochle while the Midwest men seemed to gravitate toward gin rummy, played in pairs. It was the good old boys from the South, both white and black, who enjoyed poker the most. There was usually one table of bridge players and that was the only one that mixed the genders, other than Violet who flitted from table to table and sat down wherever there was an empty seat, not caring what game it was, as long as it was one of the men's tables.

Homer played the piano for a while, but it was tiring for him to concentrate too long on keeping his hands still. He couldn't join any of the games because he couldn't hold the cards. Malcolm had offered to hold the cards for him, but Homer declined. He wasn't ready for that, yet. So he sat and watched the poker games and remarked openly on what he considered to be stupid plays. He got away with it because most of the players were too absorbed in their cards to notice, and those that did notice, were at least kind enough to let it alone. George, however, retorted with snide comments.

Malcolm was stacking the chairs and folding up the tables that afternoon when George re-entered the community room to watch baseball. 'You know, George, you don't have to talk to Homer the way you do. Put yourself in his shoes."

George glowered at Malcolm and exploded. "That's not my problem. Why does he have to sit with us if he's not playing? And he isn't exactly keeping his opinions to himself."

"I know, but he wants to feel part of the game. It must be awful to be deteriorating and be unable to do the things you used to do."

"Welcome to old age. You wouldn't know about that, but we all deal with it all the time."

"That's different. You know that."

George grumbled and turned on the television. Malcolm looked up at the screen and there was a news item about a place called Rock Steady Boxing, a gym that claimed to use boxing techniques to slow and reverse the symptoms of Parkinson's. George was about to turn the station when Malcolm yelled out, "Wait! Don't turn it yet."

George was startled and stopped in his tracks. He had never heard Malcolm raise his voice before. Malcolm hustled closer to the television and watched the rest of the story. When a commercial came on, he went to one of the computers to search for Rock Steady Boxing. He scrolled down the list of locations but found nothing in Venice or Santa Monica. The closest gyms were about an hour away. "Damn."

George, meanwhile, had found the game and sat down to watch and yell at the television. His fellow Dodger fans soon joined him. Their outbursts didn't disturb Malcolm, though. He was too absorbed in finding out everything he could about his new idea.

16

MALCOLM HURRIED HOME FOR A SHOWER BEFORE LEAVING FOR THE CAFE. He didn't see Nick and wasn't sure if he was in his bedroom or if he had actually dared to go out. His laptop was still sitting on the table, so Malcolm wasn't concerned that he had left altogether.

Malcolm worked late. It was tiring but fruitful, so worth it. He fell into bed, exhausted, knowing he had a long day Saturday, even though he wasn't working at the residence. Now that he had that job, his Saturday mornings were spent at the homeless table on the boardwalk and his Saturday afternoons at the children's hospital. And then he had to go to work at the cafe Saturday night. Another day passed without Nick and Malcolm running into each other.

He had promised Charlie that he would also work Sunday morning at the table. He didn't always work Sundays because he wanted at least one day to himself. But Charlie had asked if he could help him out. He had to attend a church service because the pastor had wanted him to meet with some of the deacons and church members. They wanted to sponsor Charlie's work as a church-affiliated cause. That would mean money and volunteers that Charlie could count on as an ongoing resource. If this worked out, it would also relieve Malcolm of his time commitment and at this point, Malcolm would welcome that.

It was a beautiful day at the beach, so when Charlie came to relieve him at one, Malcolm decided to take a walk down the boardwalk. He arrived at Muscle Beach and saw Savali on one of the machines. She looked particularly masculine as she grunted through her workout. But when she noticed him watching her, she jumped down off the apparatus and sauntered over to him. She wore shorts and a muscle shirt and her upper arms were defined and taut. But in her enigmatic style, her face was skillfully made up and her hair was smooth and styled and Malcolm felt his body stir with excitement.

"Hey Jimmy boy, you coming to work out?"

"Jimmy boy?"

"Bond. James Bond."

Malcolm laughed. "Oh, that. No. I was volunteering at the homeless table and thought I'd take a walk."

"Well, come on. I'll show you some good exercises."

"No thanks. I'll just watch you."

"Oh, c'mon. You need to put some meat on those bones."

"I can't stay. I'll get a bite and then I need to get home."

"Then let's go get a bite." Savali went back inside the fence to get her gym bag before Malcolm had a chance to protest, not that he was going to. "Where do you want to eat?" she asked as she took his arm and started walking.

Malcolm stiffened when she touched him, but tried not to show any reaction. "I don't know. You choose."

"Okay. Let's go to the Ale House. I feel like a beer."

"Sure." Malcolm didn't usually drink in the afternoon, but he wanted to please her. They walked with her arm still through his and Malcolm was more than comfortable with her keeping it there. He was falling hard for her. "So do you live here?" Malcolm asked. "I mean Venice? Near the boardwalk?"

"Yeah. Just up the street. How about you?"

"Off Rose up past Lincoln."

"Near Whole Earth?"

"Yes. Real close."

"Then we're neighbors sometimes."

"Sometimes?"

"I live in my van. Sometimes I park it in the Whole Earth parking lot."

Malcolm stumbled and looked at her. "You live in your van?"

"What? You think I can afford to rent an apartment with the wages they pay me at that place? Hah! Not in Venice."

"I guess that's true. But your van?"

"It's cool. I like it. It's cozy."

"Is it like fully equipped?"

"You mean you want to know if it has a bathroom and a shower?"

Malcolm grinned. "Yeah."

"It does. A little funky, but everything works."

Malcolm shook his head. "You just keep on surprising me, Savali."

"That's what I do." She grinned back. They arrived at the Ale House and found a place to sit outside. "You'll have to come see my abode sometime."

"I'd like to. It definitely sounds cool."

At that point the server arrived with menus. "I know what I want," Savali said, handing him back her menu. "I'll have a quinoa bowl and a White Dog IPA."

Malcolm glanced quickly at the menu and ordered a vegetarian wrap. "And I'll try the White Dog too."

"So you rent an apartment?" Savali continued with her questioning.

"No. I have a house."

Her eyes widened. "You own a house in Venice? You bought that with tip money? Jeez."

"Hardly. I inherited it."

"So you're a trust-fund baby?"

"It's not what you think. It's a small bungalow and it was left to me by my foster mother who ended up adopting me."

"That sounds more like it."

"And what's your story?" Malcolm might finally get some answers to all his questions about her, if she was truly a she.

The waiter set the beers down on the table and Savali took a long swig from hers. Malcolm wasn't sure if that was to waste time or if it was just for emphasis. He waited for her to answer, which took a few minutes. "You really want to know, don't you?" Malcolm nodded and took another swig. "You want to know if I'm a male or a female?"

Malcolm nodded and waited for an answer. When none was forthcoming after a couple of minutes passed, he answered, "If you want to talk about it. You don't have to."

"Of course I don't have to."

"I'm sorry. It's none of my business. Forget it."

Savali took another large sip. "Neither."

Malcolm stared at her. "Neither what?"

"Neither male nor female. Or both. Depends how you want to look at it. Have you ever heard of Fa'afafine?"

"No. What is it?"

Again, Savali took a sip and stayed quiet. The waiter brought their food. "Two more?"

Malcolm looked at Savali, but she didn't respond. "Not right now," he answered.

They ate silently for several minutes. Malcolm decided he should wait for Savali to share whatever she wished to. If it were nothing, then it would be an awkward lunch. But she finally spoke after eating half her meal. "Third gender is a classification in lots of cultures. Fa'afafine is the name for Samoans who don't identify male or female, specifically."

Malcolm thought about that for a minute. He still didn't feel like his question was answered. "Okay."

"But that's not me, exactly."

"I see." He wasn't sure how to respond. He waited to see if more information was imminent.

"Third gender is not transgender, transsexual, or intersexual. It's different."

"So that's how you label yourself? Third gender?"

"Some cultures recognize five or more genders. Native Americans use a term called two-spirit. There are lots of variations. I don't like to label myself at all."

"So what pronoun do you use?"

"I use 'I' and 'me'."

Okay, what pronoun would you like others to use to refer to you?"

She smiled. "You?"

"C'mon, Savali. You know what I mean, 'he' or 'she'?"

"A lot of folks like 'they'."

"Is that what you want us to use?"

"What do you want to use?"

Malcolm sighed. "You can be so aggravating sometimes!"

"I know. It's what makes me so lovable." She patted his arm. "I don't care, honestly. Just do what makes you comfortable. I'm comfortable with any and all of them."

"Well I'd prefer to use 'she'."

"Then use it for now. I'll let you know if I change my mind." She laughed.

"Is that true, or are you just pulling my leg again?"

"If I were to pull at any part of your body, Malcolm, it would not be at a restaurant table."

Malcolm didn't answer this last sexual innuendo. He finished his food and drink without talking. Anyway, he sensed that Savali was done discussing gender identity for the moment. "I'd like to see your van sometime."

"You want to see it now?"

Malcolm shrugged. "Sure." He took out his wallet and waved down the server to bring the check.

"You paying?"

"Sure."

"Aren't you the gentleman."

"Yes." He started to make a joke about him being of the male gender, but thought better of it. The waiter brought the check and Malcolm paid. They left the restaurant and strangely enough, Savali took Malcolm's arm as if it was the most natural thing to do.

Savali started to walk up Rose Avenue, pulling Malcolm's arm to follow her. "Are we going to Whole Foods? Is that where you're parked?" Malcolm asked.

"Nah. On weekends my friends at Gold's Gym let me park in their lot."

"So you work out there too?"

"Sometimes."

They turned south on Main Street and soon approached Google's Los Angeles headquarters. "This building is so incredible. It must be cool to work here."

"So why don't you apply for a job?" Savali asked.

"As a what? I'm not a computer geek."

"They must need other people too."

"Why don't you apply then?"

"I wasn't the one who thought it would be cool to work here. I like my life, thanks."

"Gee, sorry, didn't mean to imply you had a crappy life."

Savali shook her head and gave him a roguish smile. "Oh, Malcolm. Stop taking everything so seriously." She squeezed his arm. "You worry too much about everything and everyone."

She was right. In fact, he now remembered that he was going to look into Rock Steady Boxing for Homer. And they were on their way to Gold's Gym. Perfect.

17

SAVALI LET GO OF MALCOM'S ARM WHEN THEY GOT TO THE PARKING LOT. He wasn't sure if it was deliberate or subconscious. Or maybe it was neither and he was putting too much into it. The parking lot was packed as they walked toward a brown, nondescript, older Dodge van, parked in the farthest corner. There were no windows on the sides and its rear window had curtains, making it the only reason someone could mistake it for a house as opposed to a delivery truck.

"Welcome to my abode," Savali said as she unlocked the rear door and opened it.

A futon was folded up against one side, looking like a couch, with a couple of pillows and a quilt folded on top. Along the other side of the van were wooden cubes stacked up to the ceiling. These crates were solid wood rather than slatted and they had tops. "Do you just roll out the futon to sleep?" Malcolm asked.

"It depends. I move the boxes across the floor and put the futon on top if I want more room sleeping. Mostly I just lie on it like a couch."

He noticed an empty pail in the corner. "Is that for the middle of the night?" he grinned.

"The gym's open five am to eleven pm and Whole Earth is open six thirty to ten. But sometimes I have to park on a street. That's when the bucket comes in handy."

"Do you have a stove?"

"Camp stove. I can't really use it in the parking lot."

"Does Annabel know you live in a van?"

Savali shrugged. "I don't know. Violet knows though. She lets me use her shower during the week and her kitchen if I want to cook something and bring it back to the van. I can shower at the gym when I'm here."

"Violet? That's cool." He noticed an ice chest and a propane camp stove. There was a pole hanging on the side of the van across from the futon with dresses, jackets, and men's suits hanging from it.

"So are all your questions answered now?"

He wanted to ask about the men's suits. Malcolm had assumed Savali lived alone in the van, but maybe he was wrong. Maybe she had a significant other after all. Maybe he'd been wrong about everything. But he decided not to ask. "I guess so," he finally replied. "Can you introduce me to your friends at the gym? I want to ask them something."

"What's that?"

"It's for Homer. I heard about this thing called Rock Steady Boxing. It's supposed to help people with Parkinson's."

"Hmmm. Interesting. Sure. C'mon."

She led him out of the van and locked the door. Malcolm noticed a couple of other vans parked in the lot as they crossed it. "I guess others have the same idea as you."

"Brilliant, Jimmy B. Let's see, if you live in a van what are you lacking? Oh yeah: toilets and showers. And what do you know? That's what gyms provide. You are definitely the world's best detective!"

Malcolm frowned. "Do you ever stop?"

"Stop what?"

"Being sarcastic."

"Yes. But you're such an easy target. Nice guys always are." They reached the door to the gym and Savali led him inside. "Hey, Jacob!

Is Dwight around?" she asked the man at the front desk.

"Nah. It's Sunday."

Savali turned to Malcolm. "Sorry."

"Maybe you could ask him about it tomorrow?"

"I guess. But I don't usually stay during the week."

"Well, can't you call him tomorrow then?"

"Man, Malcolm!"

"If it's too much trouble I can call him myself, but you'll need to give me his number."

"I'll ask him. Don't worry about it. I'm going to take advantage of the luxurious bathroom facilities while I'm here." She walked toward the locker room.

Malcolm turned to Jacob. "Alright if I look around?"

"Sure. You want to join?"

"Uh. Maybe. Yeah." Malcolm strolled around the club, watching the weightlifters and the spinners, and peeking through the door to a Yoga class. He wandered around looking for a boxing area and noticed a personal trainer working with one woman, kickboxing. What he didn't see was a boxing ring or even one boxing bag. He noticed Savali coming out of the locker room and walked briskly over to her. "Never mind about asking Dwight. I don't think there's any boxing here."

"I could have told you that. I thought you just wanted to ask him about it. Like where he might suggest going."

"Oh. Well, okay. I guess you can ask him that."

"Oh, Malcolm. You really are too cute sometimes."

Malcolm smiled wanly. It was too tiring staying on his toes and trying to be witty with Savali. "I think I'm going home now. It was a good lunch and I enjoyed visiting with you and seeing your van."

"Oh." Savali looked genuinely surprised. "Oh," she repeated. "Okay. I thought we might hang out a while. Well, maybe sometime you could invite me to your house."

Had he hurt her feelings? He didn't even realize that she had feelings capable of being hurt; she was so self-assured. But, he really did want to get home and see Nick. "Yeah. That would be nice."

She looked at him expectantly, but Malcolm didn't bite. "See ya tomorrow morning at work."

Savali managed a coy smile. "Bye Malcolm."

He left the gym and speed walked the few blocks home. Nick sat in the living room, typing on his laptop, and looked up when Malcolm entered the house. "Where the hell have you been?"

"I could say the same thing," Malcolm answered.

"Well, I'm here now."

"Where did you go? Have you been gone all weekend?"

"I have to tell you where I am every minute? Is that a parameter for letting me stay here?"

"No. I was just wondering. You don't have to tell me. But since you are staying here and your brother, the drug trafficker, is looking for you, and you are hiding from him, it does make the circumstances a bit risky for me."

Nick grumbled under his breath. "Well, I need some help. I thought I'd call my mother. But it has to be untraceable. I need one of those throwaway phones."

"You mean a burner phone?"

"Yes! For Christ's sake Malcolm! Of course I mean a burner phone! You think I'm going to hang on to it after I use it? Anthony's not a dummy."

"And you need me to go buy one for you?"

"I have no money. Remember?" Nick was getting agitated. "Look, if you don't want to get involved I'll figure something else out."

"I'll buy you the phone, Nick. It'll take me awhile. I have to find a store that sells one and I don't have a car." This was not the way Malcolm wanted to spend the rest of his day off. "Should I pick up some dinner while I'm out?"

"Whatever you want. And thanks, Malcolm." Maybe just hearing a thank you from Nick made it worthwhile.

Nick was on his computer when Malcolm got back several hours later with the phone and some Thai food. "I'll set the phone up for you after we eat. Could you get some plates and silverware?"

Nick brought the forks and plates into the dining room and sat down while Malcolm opened the containers. "What the hell is this?"

"Pad Thai, chicken satay, red curry and rice."

Nick made a face as he spooned some onto his plate. He picked up the stick of chicken satay. "How do I eat this?"

"Well, first of all, here's some peanut sauce you can dip it in. Then just take it off the stick with your teeth."

Nick tried it and shrugged. "Not bad."

Malcolm smiled. "I bought you sixty minutes for the phone. You can put more minutes on if you need to."

"I told you! I'm throwing it away after I call her!"

"Okay. I just wasn't sure how much to get."

"Sixty minutes is more than enough."

"I ran into Savali today. She showed me her van. Did you know she lived in a van?"

"Yep."

Malcolm was surprised. He didn't think it was the kind of thing she would have shared with the residents. "She said that Violet lets her use her shower and stove sometimes."

"I know."

They finished eating and cleaned up. Malcolm took the phone and showed Nick how to use it. "Did you get the number for the hospital yet?"

"I have it on my computer."

Malcolm sat on the sofa, waiting for Nick to dial the number. Nick stared at him and didn't make a move. It finally dawned on Malcolm that maybe Nick wanted to be alone to make the call. "I have some stuff to do." Malcolm left Nick in the living room and went to his room to Google "Third Gender."

Malcolm waited an hour before emerging from his bedroom, just in case Nick used up the whole sixty minutes and was still on the phone. He found Nick sitting at the dining room table, staring out the window. "Did you talk to her?" Malcolm asked as he sat down across from Nick.

"She was sleeping."

"Oh. That's too bad. Well, you can try again later."

"I talked to the nurse."

"What did she say?"

"It's a he and he said that she sleeps most of the time."

"Oh sorry. He. I guess I'm as guilty as anyone of making assumptions."

"I thought you'd be more politically correct."

"Sorry to disappoint you. Did *he* say any more about how she's doing?"

"She's old and sick. What else does he have to say?"

"Are you going to try to call again?"

"Yeah, but I have to figure out a time when no one else is there with her."

"Maybe you should make some kind of agreement with the nurse."

"Thanks for the tip." Nick sighed. "I know what I'm doing, Malcolm."

Malcolm got up and went back to his room. Probably best to leave Nick alone for now. Anyway, he wanted to get back to his research on third gender. He found that many cultures believed in more than one gender. Even traditional Judaism categorized six different genders. Native Americans acknowledged five: female, male, two-spirit female, two-spirit male and transgendered before the Europeans came. Hawaii, like Samoa, still recognizes a gender that is not exclusively male or female. Malcolm was mesmerized, watching YouTube videos and reading research papers. He was so engrossed he didn't hear Nick knocking on his door and looked up to find Nick standing in the doorway.
"Oh, I didn't hear you."

"I've been knocking. Sorry to barge in."

"No problem. What's up?"

"I talked to the nurse again."

"And?"

"He said she's on hospice and it could be a week or a month, but not much longer than that."

Malcolm was amazed that Nick was sharing all this with him and that he showed some emotional angst. "Did the nurse say she had a lot of visitors?"

"Yeah. But he said when patients are dying they suspend the rules."

"So you could visit in the middle of the night and no one would be there or care?"

"Something like that."

"Do you want to go?"

Nick stared at Malcolm. "How would I get there?"

"Airplane?"

"Are you kidding? You don't think my brother's got ways of finding people? He has connections everywhere."

"You mean he could find out if you bought an airplane ticket?"

"You are so naive. Of course."

"Then why hasn't he found you here?"

"He probably doesn't suspect you." Nick didn't sound altogether convinced.

"Is that why you came to me for help?"

"It crossed my mind. What? Did you think it was because you're my best friend?"

Malcolm shrugged. "More like your only one." Nick laughed but Malcolm wasn't sure why. Was he laughing because Malcolm was right? "Well, then I guess you can't buy an airplane ticket. Hey, if your brother has so many connections that he could find you, don't you have the same connections to help you get a plane ticket under the radar?"

"Jesus Christ Malcolm! I'm on the run from them. Have you forgotten? I'd be playing into their hands. They want me dead. Get that into your thick skull. They're all afraid I'll rat them out."

"Okay. Okay. I get it." But Malcolm was so rattled that he couldn't keep the questions from pouring out. "So what are you going to do?"

"You'll be the first to know if I figure it out. You want me out of here?"

"No," he replied, rubbing his head. "Just trying to help."

"Well, you're not helping by asking me all these questions. Why don't you go to bed or something."

"Huh? Well, okay," Malcolm replied coldly. "Good night, Nick."

Nick waved his hand dismissively. "Pleasant dreams."

145

18

NICK WAS ASLEEP WHEN MALCOLM LEFT FOR WORK THE NEXT MORNING. That was just fine with Malcolm. He had no interest in continuing the conversation with Nick. These weren't some petty criminals. This was the big time and Malcolm was a little scared. He also avoided Savali when he got to Moss House. He thought he could figure out what he wanted to do and where he wanted to go with little drama. He had two jobs that didn't take a lot of extra time or extra work or even extra thought. And yet, his life had become much more complicated since starting this activities coordinator job.

Homer was practicing the piano, George was reading the newspaper, while a few others were reading or chatting in the community room. Malcolm gave them all a hearty good morning and started setting up the tables for Arts and Crafts Day. A couple of women came in with paint, brushes, easels, and paper. Two more women arrived with cardstock and bags of seashells, buttons, sea glass pieces, and dried flowers to make collages. All Malcolm had to do was set up and clean up at the end. He had used his own money to buy some of the materials and had sent an email to Annabel to be reimbursed. She said she would have it added to his paycheck.

After setting up, he tried to entice some of the men to join the class. He was successful with a couple of them willing to paint. He had no male takers for the collage making, however. Maybe it was the "feminine" materials. All his reading yesterday got him thinking about non-binary gender and how much better it would be if we believed as other cultures do. Just at that moment Savali entered the room.

"Hey, Secret Agent Man!"

"Hey, Savali."

"You got a minute?"

He nodded and followed her back to the office. They sat down across the desk from each other. "What's up?" he asked.

"I got a call from Nick's brother, Anthony."

"So?"

"He seems to think you know where Nick is."

Malcolm stayed silent. He wasn't sure whether to lie and say he didn't know, make up a story to steer Anthony into a different direction or tell Savali the truth. He knew damn well, of course, that his silence would give him away. "And if I do, why would I tell Anthony?"

"I'm just letting you know. I'm not asking you to tell me anything. I just don't want you to be in any kind of trouble. I'm looking out for you."

"Thanks, but I'm capable of looking out for myself."

"Hey, this isn't about emasculation. This is about it probably not being a good idea to get yourself mixed up with Nick's family."

"But I'm already mixed up in this."

"I know. Me too, I guess."

Malcolm stood up to leave before he was tempted to tell Savali the whole story and drag her deeper into the situation. "I need to get back and see if they're ready to clean up."

Savali called out to him as he walked out of the office, "Want to have lunch today?"

Malcolm stopped but didn't answer right away. He turned to look at her. "Only if we don't talk about Nick."

"Fair enough," Savali answered.

Lunch hardly turned out that way. They had barely sat down at the Sidewalk Cafe on the boardwalk when the words poured out of Malcolm. "Nick is at my house. He's called his mother and wants to go visit her, but he can't fly. Anthony would find him if he got a plane ticket."

"Then how would he see her without seeing other members of his family?"

"So you know Nick's story?"

"Mostly I just figured it out. It wasn't hard. Nick had told me a little and then when I met Anthony, it was pretty easy to unravel. He really looks the part, a lot more than Nick."

"Maybe Nick changed his look."

She laughed. "He's quite a chameleon."

"You would know a lot about chameleons."

A sardonic twist passed over Savali's unadorned lips. "So how's he going to get to San Francisco? Bus? Hitchhike?"

"I don't know. He's scared, Savali. He won't say so, but he is."

The waitress came with their food and set it down. Savali ate several bites of her salad and then sat back in her chair. "Maybe we should take him."

Malcolm almost choked on his burger. "Huh?"

"In my van." Malcolm continued to eat, letting what Savali said sink in. "I was planning to bring the van in for a couple of problems anyway. I'll have them check it out to see if it could make it. The van hasn't left Venice in quite a while. It needs some exercise." Malcolm laughed. "I'm serious. The engine could probably use some freeway and open road driving."

"When? And how could we both be gone from the residence at the same time?"

Savali looked hard at him and shook her head. "You think we are so indispensable that the place couldn't run without us?"

He smiled. "I guess it wouldn't be a problem."

"I'm not talking about being gone a long time. Neither of us can afford to not be working."

"True." Malcolm enjoyed the idea of spending a few days with Savali. He might finally be able to figure her out. Or him. They finished their lunch, both lost in their own thoughts. "When would we leave?" Malcolm asked when the server had removed their plates.

"Obviously we'd have to go soon. And it won't take long for Anthony to find him at your house. I can bring the van in right now. You go back and I'll call you."

"Are we talking about leaving tonight? I mean I'd have to let the cafe know. And Annabel of course." Malcolm was starting to feel like a real flake.

"Probably not tonight. Maybe we could go tomorrow if the van checks out."

"I'm actually pretty decent with cars. I learned some mechanics as an engineer in the army."

"Well then, maybe I shouldn't bother to bring it in. If something goes wrong, my knight in shining armor will save the day."

"I didn't think you needed one."

Savali passed a hand over her well-developed upper arm. "Well, someone mechanically inclined is always handy."

"Look," Malcolm sighed. "Nick needs to visit in the middle of the night when none of the other relatives will be there."

"If we leave right after work, we'll get there in the middle of the night."

"Okay, but we need to talk to Nick first and see if this is, in fact, what he wants."

"I thought you said he wanted to visit her."

"Well, not in so many words."

"What? I don't get you, Malcolm."

"Well I sure as hell don't understand you either!"

"What is wrong with you?" Savali shook her head in disgust. "Maybe I should drive him myself."

"Savali, just let me talk to Nick. And you can still take the van in and let them tell you what needs fixing. Then I can see if it's something I can do."

"Well, I'd be a fool to pass up that offer." Savali rose abruptly. "I'll let you know what they say." At that, Savali walked off. Malcolm paid the bill, looked at the time on his phone and decided he had time to go home and talk to Nick before going back to Moss House. Probably no one would even notice he was gone. Or care.

He found Nick in the living room.

"What the hell are you doing here?" demanded Nick.

"Nice to see you too."

"Very funny. Aren't you supposed to be at work?"

"I'm on my lunch break." Malcolm realized that in order to discuss the idea of driving Nick to San Francisco, he'd have to admit to spilling the beans to Savali. Certainly Nick trusted Savali, but he also knew that his brother had been in touch with her. Malcolm wasn't sure if Nick would be angry, scared, or simply wouldn't care at all. "Did you reach your mother yet?"

"No. But I spoke to the nurse again. He seems to be a good guy. I told him that he's not to tell any other relative that he spoke to me and he seemed to understand."

"Well, if the rest of your relatives look like your brother, the nurse can probably understand who they are."

"You're a regular Hardy boy, aren't you?"

"I'm sorry." Malcolm found himself saying he was sorry an awful lot lately.

"So why are you home, Malcolm?"

"I wanted to talk to you. I, um, told Savali about your predicament."

Nick started sputtering, "You what?!!"

For once, Malcolm plowed on rather than try to appease Nick. "Hey, she just wants to help you see your mother, too. We thought we could drive you up to San Francisco in her van."

This shut Nick up. He finally spoke. "When?"

"Savali is taking her van to the mechanic just now to see if there are any problems that need to be addressed before taking off. We thought maybe tomorrow afternoon so you could get there in the middle of the night."

"I don't know."

"I need to get back to work. And I need to let the manager of the cafe know tonight if I'll be gone a couple of days. So decide and tell me when I get back this afternoon. Okay?"

Nick didn't answer; he just stared off into a corner.

19

THE AFTERNOON PASSED QUICKLY. Several of the residents needed help with their computers and phones so Malcolm watched a bunch of videos on YouTube to get solutions to technical problems. He wasn't that much of a computer whiz, but he was curious and persistent. He learned a lot, though, because things kept going wrong and he had to right them. It was how he learned mechanics when he was in the army. Hard use and extreme conditions caused many problems.

Savali came back with the news that the mechanic couldn't go over her van until the following morning. "So where will you sleep tonight?" Malcolm asked her.

"I don't know. I'll figure something out. I would have just slept in it anyway, but they said there was no place to leave it outside the shop without being ticketed or towed."

"You can sleep on my sofa if you want."

Savali paused. She cocked her head to one side and smiled. "Thanks."

What was she saying with that coy look of hers? Did she expect to sleep somewhere else in his house? Damn she was maddening! "I'll tell Nick you'll be coming when I go home to shower and change."

"I'll just go home with you." She turned abruptly and went back to the office.

Malcolm returned to his "repair shop" where Homer was waiting for him. "Hey, Malcolm. I figured it was time for me to learn how to work this damn thing."

Homer had an old iPhone in his hand. He was shaking pretty badly and Malcolm took it from him quickly, afraid that it would fall to the floor and be unusable. "This is an old one. How long have you had it?" Malcolm asked as he plugged it in and turned it on.

"I don't know. Savali gave it to me several months ago. I guess she got a new one and gave me her old one."

"It looks like a 4."

"What do you mean a 4?"

"An iPhone 4. That's the model."

"Oh."

"If it works, you'll be fine, but if it breaks, I doubt you'd be able to get it fixed. I think it's probably obsolete."

"Well, I don't need anything fancy. I just want to use it as a phone and to look up stuff. Can I still do that?"

"I think so. Let's see." The phone booted up. "Seems fine. Did Savali say it was working well when she gave it to you?"

"Yeah. She just said she bought the latest model."

Malcolm laughed. "It's probably not the latest model anymore."

"Well, how do I do it? Never had one of these before. You taught me about Google on the computer. So how can I do it on this phone?"

"First of all you have to sign up with a service like Verizon or AT&T and get a phone number."

"How much is that going to cost?"

"'I'm not sure."

"Where do I do that?"

"At one of their stores." Malcolm remembered how far he had to walk to get to the store to buy Nick that throwaway phone. "I'll help you find one. That's the first step." He went to one of the resident computers to find the closest place.

"It's more than two miles to the closest phone store. Can you take a cab?"

"I'll ask George to drive me."

"George has a car?"

"No, but he has a buddy who lets him use his sometimes."

"I didn't know you were good pals with George."

"He's not who you think he is when you first meet him. Under that rough exterior is a kind man."

Malcolm smiled. That made his day: George, a kind man. Nick writes poetry. You just never know . . . "That's good to know." And that gave Malcolm an idea. "Where is George? Have you seen him today?"

"He was here earlier. Is today the day he goes to the gym? What day is it?"

"It's Monday."

"Then George should be around. He goes to the gym on Tuesdays and Thursdays. Those are the days he gets to use his friend's car."

"Great. Then he could bring you tomorrow. I'll go look for him. Wait here."

Malcolm went upstairs to George's apartment and knocked. He glanced at Nick's door while he waited, wondering if Nick needed some things for their road trip. At least he wouldn't be holed up in a stranger's house for a couple of days. Maybe being on the road would give him a new outlook and shake off the morbid thoughts of family. They really couldn't kill their own kin, could they? George didn't answer the door, so Malcolm went back downstairs.

"Yoo-hoo, Malcolm," Violet's voice rang out as he got to the community room.

"Hi Violet. What can I do for you?"

Violet raised her eyebrows and winked. "I don't know, Malcolm, but I'd love to find out."

Malcolm shook his head and walked away, scanning the room for George or Homer or both. He saw Homer at the piano. "George wasn't in his apartment."

"I'll talk to him later," Homer said.

Malcolm was disappointed. He wanted to talk to George about Rock Steady Boxing for Homer. "I'm going to be gone a couple of days."

"Okay. Where are you going?" Homer asked.

"To San Francisco."

"We can ask Savali to set up the room for music in the morning."

"Well, actually, Savali is going also. I'll ask Jose to do it."

"You and Savali huh?"

Oh crap. He said too much. It was no one's business where he was going and now he was afraid that he might have compromised Nick. Suppose Anthony came by and asked for Savali and Homer told him. "Uh, could you keep it to yourself please, Homer?"

"Sure. Loose lips sink ships. Won't tell a soul."

"Thanks." Malcolm looked for Jose. There wasn't that much to get ready for music and he was there anyway teaching guitar. He would be sure not to tell Jose where they were going or that they would be together. It could just be a coincidence that he and Savali were both absent on the same days.

PE on Wednesday would be a different story. Besides needing to move all the furniture around, Savali wouldn't be there to teach Yoga and Pilates. Now he wanted to find George more than ever. If he was really a kind man then maybe he'd step up to the plate and take over the 11 to 12 slot and teach boxing. That would be a perfect solution if he'd agree. He went to the office to find Savali. "Hey, have you told Annabel yet?"

"Told her what?" Savali asked.

"That we'd both be gone for a couple of days."

"I told her I'd be gone. You'll need to take care of your own business."

She was more on the ball than he was. She had already figured out that it wouldn't be wise to tell anyone that they'd be together. "I meant that you'd be gone. I'll call her myself. Is she going to come and work here?"

Savali shrugged. "Not my problem. That's why she gets the big bucks."

Malcolm nodded. "I thought I'd ask Jose to set up the room for the classes for me tomorrow and Wednesday. And I was hoping to ask George to teach boxing on Wednesday in place of your class."

"Good luck with that. But Malcolm, you really don't have to worry about it. They will survive a week without their workout. They spent many Wednesdays doing nothing before you came."

"I know. But I want to keep the momentum going. If they stop, they might not come back."

"You're such a mother hen!" Savali chuckled and went back to the office.

Malcolm took out his phone and saw that he had to leave or risk being late for the cafe. He'd call Annabel as he walked home. "Hey Savali!" he called out to her. She turned around. "I have to leave."

"I'll be over later. I still have some work to do."

"Well, you'll need the address."

"I have it on your application."

"Oh man, I have to let Jose know about setting up. Is he still here?"

"I'll take care of it, Malcolm. Go ahead. You'll be late. Just make sure you let Nick know I'm coming, so he doesn't freak out."

"Okay. See you later . . . much later."

"Yeah, yeah, yeah." She waved dismissively.

"Oh, maybe you could bring some dinner home for Nick."

"Maybe." She went back to her office. Nice. Well, at least there was cereal left.

He jogged home, leaving a voice mail for Annabel and rushed into the bathroom to shower. Malcolm knocked on Nick's door, as he was about to leave. "You in there, Nick?"

Nick opened the door, still dressed in the clothes he had on from yesterday. Malcolm then remembered he had thought about bringing something clean for him to wear from his apartment. "I'm going to work. Savali is sleeping here tonight while her van is being readied for the trip. We'll leave as soon as we can." And at that moment, Malcolm realized that they wouldn't be leaving in the morning at any rate and he could be at work the next day after all. "I guess it won't be until tomorrow afternoon at the earliest. Do you want me to bring you some clean clothes from your apartment?"

"No. Don't go in there. Anthony might have it booby-trapped."

"Seriously?"

"Yes. Seriously. I'm fine."

"Maybe you can fit into something of mine. Go ahead and look in my closet and dresser and see what you can find." Nick shrugged. He looked like hell. Like he hadn't slept. "Were you able to talk to your mother?"

"I didn't try again."

"You do want to go, right?"

Nick shrugged. "I don't know. I guess it doesn't matter."

"What do you mean it doesn't matter? Your mother is dying and you won't ever see her again! She's your mother even if you don't approve of what she's done with her life!"

"Jesus, Malcolm. Why do you have such a bug up your ass about my mother?"

"My mother died when I was fourteen! I'd give anything to have her as long as you have yours!" Malcolm stalked out and slammed the door.

He just went through the motions at the restaurant. At closing he quickly finished his usual tasks, told his manager that he wouldn't be back until Friday, and left. Despite his decisiveness, Malcolm felt like things were spiraling out of control.

20

SAVALI WAS CURLED UP ON THE SOFA, DRESSED IN GRAY SWEATS, WHEN MALCOLM OPENED THE FRONT DOOR. He tiptoed through the living room and was about to enter his bedroom when she called to him. "I'm awake."

He went back into the living room and sat down on a chair opposite her. "Hey."

"Nick wasn't too happy with what I brought him for dinner. He barely ate. I thought he'd like some nice Italian food."

"It probably wasn't the food. He seemed pretty depressed when I talked to him earlier."

"Well, that's too bad. At least I feel great. My van only needs a couple of hundred dollars worth of work and it'll be finished tomorrow by noon."

"You thought there would be more wrong with it?"

"Yep. He said it needed tires but it could wait."

"Good news. Then I guess we're all set for the big trip."

"Big trip! Ha! Four hundred miles isn't a big trip. When was the last time you were out of Los Angeles?"

Malcolm thought a while. "I don't know. A year or two?"

"Finally, a vacation!"

"This is hardly a vacation. Drive up to San Francisco, sit in a hospital waiting room and then drive back?"

Savali stared at him. "That's it? We're not going to do anything in San Francisco?"

"What would we do? And we need to get back to work."

"You really do think that we are indispensable, don't you? I, for one, don't intend to spend the rest of my life answering phones and filing papers in a stupid senior residence."

Malcolm didn't want to think about all this right now. He stood. "I'm going to bed."

"How about we take our excursion a little further up the coast?"

"How much further?"

"To Oregon."

"Oregon?"

"Look." She took out her phone and pulled up a page and handed it to Malcolm. He read aloud. "Oregon court rules that 'non-binary' is a gender." He handed the phone back to her. "Non-binary?"

"It's another name for 'genderqueer'."

"Uh . . ."

"Just use your imagination," Savali prompted. "Anyway, I'd like to go up to Portland and talk to the groups up there that helped get this legislation passed. I want to work on getting it passed in California."

Malcolm sat back down, a little stunned. "Is that what you call yourself? Genderqueer? That sounds derogatory."

"It's not. But, no, that's not what I call myself." She said that a bit disdainfully. "I already told you. I don't use labels. Binary gender or genderqueer are just umbrella phrases for the whole gamut or continuum of gender identification."

Malcolm exhaled and peered out the window for a couple of minutes. "How long would we be gone?"

"I'm not sure. Maybe through the weekend? Can the restaurant live without you that long?" Malcolm grimaced. "I'm just kidding. Jeez."

"Did you mention this to Nick?" Malcolm finally asked.

"Why would he care? He's on the run anyway. He'd probably appreciate being away from Los Angeles and San Francisco. Less chance of being found."

"I guess you're right about that. I don't know, Savali. Can I think about it overnight?"

"Oh Malcolm. Be spontaneous. Focus on yourself."

"What's that supposed to mean?"

"You're a great guy. And it's nice to care about others. But sometimes I think you do it to your own detriment."

She watched him consider her words, but he said nothing. Malcolm ran his hands over his head, got up out of the chair and walked out of the room. His voice echoed in the hall, "Goodnight, Savali."

Savali shrugged to herself. "Goodnight, Malcolm." She turned onto her side and closed her eyes. She fell asleep right away on what she considered luxurious accommodations.

Malcolm, meanwhile, lay awake for a couple of hours. It was no longer about the trip that lay ahead. He pondered the last words she had said about him. He knew she was right. And the worst part was that it made his feelings for her even stronger.

Savali and Nick were both drinking coffee when Malcolm stumbled into the kitchen. "Good morning," Savali chirped as she handed him a cup of coffee. "Aren't we just like one big happy family? All having breakfast together in the kitchen before going to work."

Malcolm took a sip and nodded sleepily. He glanced at Nick who was staring out the window, ignoring both of them. Malcolm opened the refrigerator and saw it filled with milk, eggs, cheese, bacon, and butter: all the ingredients for a hearty breakfast. "You bought all this?"

"Um hum." She slipped by him and started pulling the items from the fridge. "I'll have breakfast ready in a minute. Go ahead and get dressed." She watched him turn to look at the clock. "There's plenty of time before we have to be at work," she sighed.

"Okay. Thanks." He turned to Nick. "Did Savali catch you up on her new travel plans?"

"Yeah."

Malcolm wanted to talk to Nick, but he seemed less than interested so he left to get dressed. True to her word, breakfast was on the table when he emerged from the bathroom. "Looks delicious."

"I don't get much opportunity to cook. I like to. I'll make you a rocking dinner one of these days."

Malcolm watched as Nick ate heartily. He was glad to see it. He'd been worried that Nick was depressed and not eating. Maybe he just enjoyed a home cooked meal. He probably hadn't had one since he split from his family. "That was good, Savali. Thanks." He started to clear the table.

"Nick will do that, won't you Nick? We have to get to work and you have nothing else to do while we wait for the van to be ready."

"Yeah, yeah, yeah. Go ahead," Nick grumbled.

"Are we both going to get the van?" Malcolm asked as he and Savali walked out the front door.

"I was hoping so. Then you can talk to the mechanic about what's wrong and see if we're going to make it without getting stuck somewhere."

"I thought you said it just needed a couple of hundred dollars worth?"

"Well, kind of. That fixes the critical issues."

"What do you mean?"

"Hey, man, it's an old van. It's got a few things wrong with it, okay? But this will get us on the road. And hey, you said you can fix cars."

"But I won't have proper tools and it's not like I can fix stuff on the side of the road."

"Stop worrying. It'll be fun. An adventure. Don't be such a killjoy. Maybe nothing will go wrong."

"I'm just being realistic."

She shook her head and muttered, "Spoilsport."

"Okay, okay."

"You know, Malcolm, I thought you were more upbeat than that."

"I thought I was, too."

"So what happened?"

"I'm just a little confused, I guess. I need to make some decisions."

"Like what? Whether or not to go to San Francisco for a couple of days? Come on, that's not a biggie."

He sighed. "No, Savali. That's not it."

"Are you scared?"

"Scared?"

"You know, of Nick's family."

"No." Malcolm looked away. "Not of that."

"Then what are you scared of?" she asked.

"You." Malcolm turned abruptly and rushed off.

21

THERE WAS ENOUGH TIME FOR SAVALI TO GO TO MUSCLE BEACH AND DO A SHORT WORKOUT. Malcolm welcomed the extra time to talk to Homer about George and the boxing. He and Jose were setting up the room when a spry man in his eighties with a full head of unruly white hair, peeked in the community room. "Anybody home?" he said.

Malcolm looked up. "Hi. Can I help you?"

"I got a letter that I was accepted for an apartment here. I wanted to take a look and find out when I can move in."

"The person who can help you isn't here yet. Savali should be here shortly. Come on in and have a seat," Malcolm answered.

"Savali?"

"Yes. It's a Samoan name."

"Hmm. I used to know a Savali quite a few years ago."

"I think it's a common Samoan name."

"Probably so. Well, I'll look around."

"You haven't been to Moss House before?"

"No. I've been living in New York for the last few years. I used to live in Venice."

"So you rented the apartment sight unseen?"

"My daughter lives in Los Angeles. She looked at it. I trust her opinion."

"She has good taste. This is a nice place. My name is Malcolm. I'm the activities coordinator. This is Jose, the, uh, maintenance coordinator." Malcolm grinned at Jose.

"Nice meeting you both. I'm Finn. So what activities are you coordinating?"

"Today is music. Jose teaches guitar and one of the residents, Homer, teaches piano. Tomorrow is dancing and Pilates or Yoga. Thursday is a writing group and Friday is game day. Yesterday we had arts and crafts."

"That's a lot of activities. You don't teach anything?"

"No," Malcolm answered. "I leave that up to the residents to teach each other."

"I see. You have to have put in fifty years of practice before you're good enough at something to teach it." Finn smiled. "Some kind of ten thousand hour rule?"

"That was Gladwell's idea in *Outliers*."

"So you know your books, I see."

"I like to read."

"That's good to hear. I was an English teacher for many years."

"Perfect. You can teach the writing group."

Finn laughed. "We'll see."

Just then Savali rushed in, "Malcolm, the van will be ready by noon. We can pick it up this afternoon." She looked at Finn and her mouth dropped. "Is this who I think it is? Flipper? Old Fishface?"

"It is you!" Finn and Savali hugged.

"You look exactly the same, Finn."

"After the age of sixty, all you get is more wrinkles and more aches and pains. The face and body already lost its youthful glow. You, however, look great. Still working out, I see."

Savali flexed her muscles. "Yeah, I still got it." She fluttered her eyelids and thrust her hip out.

"Always flaunting it." Finn winked at her.

"What are you doing here? Looking for me?" Savali winked back at him.

"I received a letter saying I won the lottery or something. I came to look at this prized apartment and find out when I can move in."

"Let's go to the office and I'll check it out. So, are you still living at your daughter's?"

"I moved back to New York some years ago." Savali and Finn walked out together arm in arm. Malcolm and Jose looked at each other with raised eyebrows, and then went back to setting up the room.

Homer entered, holding a pile of sheet music, his hands shaking. Malcolm rushed over to take the pile before the papers scattered all over the floor. "This is a lot of sheet music," Malcolm said as he neatened up the pile and put it on top of the piano.

"Well, everyone has their favorites that they want to learn."

Malcolm looked through the pile. "I don't know too many of these."

"You're too young."

"You're the second person today to say that."

"What do you expect at a home for old people?"

Malcolm laughed and shook his head. The residents starting trickling in, some holding guitars, and took seats at the tables. Homer and Jose always started with worksheets on music theory. The time went quickly and before long, it was time to clean up. "Hey, Homer. Did you talk to George about going to the gym with him and getting your phone?"

"Yeah. He's bringing me to the phone store this afternoon when he gets back from the gym."

"Oh. I was hoping you'd go to the gym with him."

Homer shrugged. "Nah, I can't. He goes on Tuesday morning and I teach then."

"Well you could go Thursday morning."

"I like the writing group. Don't worry about it, Malcolm." Homer patted him on the shoulder.

Malcolm shrugged. Apparently, Homer didn't find it as important as he did. Savali walked in. "Hey Malcolm. When will you be ready to go get the van?"

"I just need a few more minutes to clean up."

"Okay. Come and get me when you're ready." She and Homer both left.

Violet danced over and put her arms around Malcolm's waist. "Hi, handsome. Want to dance? I can show you the steps I'm going to teach tomorrow."

"Not now, Violet. I have to finish cleaning up."

"It'll be easy for you. You're still young enough to focus and learn quickly. It's these old folks that have a hard time concentrating."

A light bulb went off in Malcolm's head. Focus. Concentration. That's what that Rock Steady Boxing had described as being the way it helped the Parkinson's patients. It didn't have to be boxing. Maybe learning to dance could also do the trick for Homer. "Excuse me, Violet." Malcolm went to one of the computers and Googled Parkinson's and dancing. Lo and behold! Dance for PD! "Violet! Come here, would you?"

"Sure, darling. What do you need?"

He pulled up a YouTube video on Dancing for Parkinson's disease. "Could you teach Homer how to dance like this?"

She watched the video. "No problem, honey. I can teach him."

"Awesome!" Malcolm gave Violet a kiss on the cheek and went to look for Homer.

"Hey, sugar. What will you give me if I teach you how to dance?" she called after him.

Malcolm zipped by the front desk, took the steps two at a time, and knocked on Homer's apartment door. "Homer? It's Malcolm. Are you in here?"

"Hold on, Malcolm. I'm coming."

Malcolm heard a thud. "Are you okay?"

"Just give me a minute, Malcolm."

Malcolm waited more than two minutes. "Homer?"

"I'm getting there." Finally the door opened and Homer leaned on the jamb, his hands shaking uncontrollably. "Sorry Malcolm, sometimes it's slow going."

"I understand. No problem. Do you need anything? Is there something I can help you with?"

"No. I just have to learn patience. What did you want?" Homer asked.

"Have you tried dancing?"

"What do you mean? I used to dance once in a while. I was never very good at it."

"I mean for the Parkinson's. It's supposed to help a lot, like the piano. It's the concentration and the focus that makes it work. Violet is going to teach tomorrow. Will you go?"

Homer shrugged his shoulders. "I don't know. I hate to hold everyone else up. They really like to cut a rug. I'll just hold them up."

"Will you go tomorrow and try? The others can still dance their own way."

"Why don't you come get me in the morning and remind me."

"I won't be here. I'm going away for a couple of days."

"I'll wait until you get back, then. Hey, what time is it? I'm supposed to meet George for him to take me to the phone store. He wanted to do it right after he got back from the gym while he still had the car."

Malcolm took out his phone. "It's after twelve. I need to go meet Savali, too. Let's go down together." They closed the door to Homer's apartment and Malcolm held Homer's arm as they walked together down the hall.

George and Savali were both waiting at the front desk when Malcolm and Homer got there. "We were just going to send the posse out to look for you," Savali said.

"Come on, Homer. Let's go." George took Homer's arm without even a cursory acknowledgment of Malcolm.

"I'm ready." Malcolm and Savali started walking. "So, that's pretty funny that you ran into your old friend."

"Isn't it? Small world. He's a big time author. Wrote a few books, even a couple of bestsellers."

"No kidding? And he was an English teacher. He'll be great to teach the Writers Workshop. If he had bestsellers, why is he getting an apartment at Moss House? You'd think he could afford something better."

"I don't think having bestselling books guarantees you a lot of money. Anyway, he always liked the boardwalk when he lived here before."

"When is he moving in?"

"I'm not sure. He's going to start paying on the first. I told him we were going to San Francisco for a few days and he asked if he could come."

"I don't think that's a good idea for Nick. He doesn't want people to know about his family."

"Oh hell, Malcolm. You are such a worrywart. It'll be fine. Finn doesn't have to know why Nick's going to San Francisco. Finn just has a friend there he wants to see. We can drop him off and pick him up when we're done."

"I guess that'll be okay."

"C'mon. This will be a fun trip."

"Well, I don't know how Finn is, but Nick is not exactly a fun-loving person."

"Aw, don't let Nick bring you down. We'll have a good time." She took his hand. Malcolm was taken aback by her move, and started to pull his hand away, but she held it tightly.

They picked up the van, although the mechanic was wary about sending it off on a long trip. "I replaced the distributor cap, the rotor, the points, the spark plugs and wires, and did an oil change. I also replaced the air and fuel filters. That will alleviate the misfiring and the problems you had with starting. But it still needs tires and brakes and a few other things."

"Malcolm knows how to do stuff. He'll take care of any problems that arise. I'll look into getting tires and brakes when I get back."

"Maybe we should do all of it now. I'd hate to be stuck on the side of the road," Malcolm protested.

Savali shot him a look and turned back to the mechanic. "How much do I owe you?"

"Three hundred fourteen and ninety-six cents." The mechanic handed her the work order.

Savali counted out three hundred and fifteen and gave it to him. "Keep the change." He gave her the keys. "Thanks. I'll come by for some of your suggestions when we get back." She and Malcolm got in the van and drove off. She turned to Malcolm. "What are you so worried about? The brakes are fine and the tires still have some tread."

"The tires have very little tread left and he's the mechanic. He checked the brakes by taking the wheels off, so he knows whether you need brakes or not. Don't you trust him?" Malcolm asked.

"I don't trust anyone who makes money by telling people something that people can't know for themselves. I'll get brakes when they make noise or don't work."

"But then it'll cost twice as much to get them fixed."

"Here we go again. Mr. Responsibility. It's not like they're going to fail."

"How do you know that?"

"Just drop it. I don't have the money to get them fixed. Leave it at that." Malcolm was about to offer to pay for the brakes, but before he could open his mouth she said, "Malcolm, I don't want your money."

"Okay, okay. I get it."

"Good. Now, it's running fine, isn't it?"

"I didn't know how it was running before, but it is a bit loud and it could also use some shocks."

Savali just shook her head. "Are you trying to get out of going on this trip?"

"No. Why do you say that?"

"Never mind." They drove in silence for a few minutes. "I'll park at your house and we can walk back to work."

"Are we going to take off right after work?"

"Okay by me. We can check with Nick when we get to your house."

"What about Finn?"

"He said he'd be ready anytime. I'll call him and tell him to meet us at your house at five."

"I hope Nick doesn't have a cow about Finn coming along."

"He's getting a free ride to San Francisco. He can't exactly complain about the company."

"I guess you're right."

"Now you get it. I'm always right." Savali winked.

They parked in front of Malcolm's house and stopped in to tell Nick that they were planning to leave right after they got home. "What time will that get us to San Francisco?" Nick asked.

"Traffic will be horrendous at that time, so I'd guess after midnight. Isn't that what you want?" Malcolm replied.

"Yeah."

"Oh, and by the way," Savali said. "An old friend of mine is coming along. There's someone he wants to see in San Francisco, too," Savali said.

Nick looked at her, warily. "What did you tell him?"

"He doesn't know anything. Don't worry. We'll just drop him off at his buddy's and then go to the hospital."

"Hold on, Savali. We're going to drop off Finn after midnight? Is that okay with him or more specifically, his friend?" Malcolm wondered.

"Jeez, Malcolm. Don't worry about it!"

"Oh lay off, Savali." Malcolm was getting irritated. "Is it such a bad thing to think about others? Really? Sometimes I wonder about you."

"Shut up, you two. You act like twelve year olds!" Nick exclaimed.

"He's right, you know," Malcolm sighed. His emotions in relation to Savali were so jumbled.

"Well," Savali sighed as she gave Malcolm a playful poke. "Sometimes we do have to defer to our elders." Malcolm smiled and the tension was eased. Savali threw back her shoulders and gave a mock command, "Let's go back to work. We'll see you about five, Nick." She took Malcolm's hand and this time he didn't pull away. She had a way of pulling him right back in, even after exasperating him.

22

THERE WASN'T THAT MUCH LEFT OF THE AFTERNOON BY THE TIME SAVALI AND MALCOLM GOT BACK TO THE HOUSE. Finn was sitting in the living room with Nick when they entered. "So you two have met, I presume?" Malcolm said.

"What do you think?" Nick was even more cantankerous than usual.

Finn, on the other hand, was relaxed and cheerful. "Yes, we have had the pleasure of each other's company for the last half hour," he said, casting a wary eye at Nick.

"So you two are ready to go?" Malcolm asked.

"Well, it's not like I haven't had all day to get ready."

"Oh, Nick. Chill, will you?" Savali chimed in. "Hey, Finn, Malcolm's all worried that your friend won't be too happy about your arriving after midnight. Is that a problem?"

"I don't know. I haven't seen him in a long time except for an hour at the bus station some years ago. I don't have any idea what hours he keeps."

"Well, you can just hang out with me and Malcolm and then drop in on him in the morning."

"What are we going to do all night long, anyway?" Malcolm asked.

"I don't know. Find an all-night cafe? Walk on Golden Gate Bridge or in the park?"

"Have you forgotten how cold it is in San Francisco?" Malcolm added.

"Why don't I call him and see if we can all go to his house while we wait for daybreak?" Finn took out his phone and scrolled through the contacts.

"You're pretty good at that for being an old guy," Savali chuckled.

"My daughter made me learn how. I have to admit, it's been handy." Finn walked into the kitchen to make the call, while Malcolm went to his room to pack a bag and Savali went to the bathroom to get ready. Nick just paced the floor.

After about half an hour, they were all gathered in the living room with their bags. Savali had changed out of her T-shirt and jeans into a black leather skirt and lace-up, high heel boots. Malcolm tried not to notice that she looked fantastic. They walked down the block to where the van was parked. "You drive, Malcolm. Okay?" Savali asked as she opened the back door. Nick and Finn stood frozen, looking at the inside of the van.

"Where are we supposed to sit?" Nick asked.

"On the futon, duh."

"Where are the seatbelts?" Nick asked, sarcastically.

"Haha. You're as bad as Malcolm, worrying about being legal."

"Yeah, that's me! Worried about what's legal. In my day our air bags were f-ing bags of cocaine."

"Touché."

Finn's eyes bugged a little, but he merely worked on diffusing the situation. "C'mon, Nick. You and I can play cards or something back here," Finn said as he climbed in.

"You brought cards?"

"Well, no," Finn admitted. "Got any cards in this gypsy wagon, Savali?" Savali rolled her eyes.

"You really want me to drive?" Malcolm asked.

"Yeah, just until we get out of the city. I really hate driving in traffic, although right now I'm hating the baggage in back worse."

"Okay." Malcolm got into the driver's seat and took a minute to familiarize himself with the workings of the van. "Three speed shift on the column?"

"Yep. Have you driven one before?"

"I'm sure I'll get the hang of it." He turned the key. The starter clattered but the engine would not catch.

"Hey, I just paid three hundred bucks and it doesn't start?"

"It's thirty years old, Savali. Three hundred bucks doesn't make a new car."

"Hey, he's my workout buddy. He gave me a break, but at least it should start."

Malcolm tried again, goosing a bit of gas into the carburetor as the starter clattered away. The engine finally woke up, belched off the rich mixture, and fell into a fairly steady idle. There were a few bucks and subsequent complaints from the back as he got used to the play in the heavy-duty clutch. "Hey, where'd you get your license, a Cracker Jack box?" Nick called out.

"Looks like Nick beats you in the cranky old man department, Finn!" Savali called over her shoulder.

"Hey, I've mellowed in my old age," Finn answered.

"Thank God." Savali turned back around. "How does the van feel to drive, Malcolm?"

"I'm getting used to it. How many miles does it have?" he asked as he looked down at the speedometer.

"Oh, that broke many moons ago. Probably over three."

"Three hundred thousand?"

"Right, Sherlock." She turned on the radio and fiddled with the tuning knob until the hiss faded from NPR.

"So the radio works?"

"Sorta, but not after we get out of the city. Are you taking the 5 or the 101?"

Malcolm was slowly merging onto the Santa Monica Freeway, which was bumper to bumper. "I thought the 5 would be faster, although I'm not looking forward to climbing the Grapevine in this thing."

"Oh, it'll be fine." She turned around. "Say, Finn? What did your friend say about showing up at his house in the middle of the night?"

"He said no problem."

"Cool." They all sat silently as they crawled through the San Fernando Valley on the 405. By the time they got to the Grapevine, well north of the palm-fringed exurbs, it was close to seven o'clock. Traffic was much lighter now, but required even more concentration. Loaded semis crawled up the five-mile grade, while lighter trucks jousted around them at only slightly faster speeds. Cars started shooting around the van as it started to lag. Malcolm dropped the column shift into second gear and the van's demise now didn't seem so imminent. It held at forty, even though the temperature gauge started climbing. Malcolm caught Savali studying the gauges and for once felt vindicated. He just hoped the hoses and the fan belt would hold out under the pressure for the next ten minutes. "Turn on the heater," Malcolm ordered.

"But it's already warm in here."

"It'll keep the engine from overheating."

"Really?" Savali pushed the lever over some. Malcolm put his hand over hers and pushed it all the way to hot, and then his fingers reached for the other lever and pushed it all the way to defrost. Savali's fingers still lay upon the heat lever with a model's touch. As he pulled his hand back to the steering wheel, his fingers grazed hers. "Ooh," she murmured.

"That way only our head and shoulders get roasted," Malcolm said.

"Hey, it's hotter than hell back here!" Nick bellowed.

"Open your wind-wing a bit to pull some of the heat outside," Malcolm told Savali.

Savali fumbled with the latch. She never used the—what did he call them—wind wings? "I'm liking this hidden side of you."

She noticed a slight uptick in the corners of his mouth as he kept one eye on the road and the other on the dash. The temperature gauge steadied at the upper limits of normal and Malcolm relaxed a little. After a number of long minutes, the van finally crested the grade and Malcolm pushed the column shift back up to third. "There!" Malcolm grinned over at Savali. "Nothing but a roller coaster ride after this."

"Can I turn off the freakin' heat now?"

"No!" Malcolm slipped the shifter into the center and let the van coast down the first short hill. "Now it can breathe easier, too."

"Who's breathing easier?" Savali shot back, a shine of sweat now reflecting off her brow. He drove over the mountains in this manner, until the lights of the San Joaquin Valley spread out below them. "Anyone else hungry?" Savali called out.

"Yes," Nick and Finn called out in unison.

"I hope everyone likes Mexican food, 'cause that's all you're gonna find around here."

"Whatever. Let's just get somewhere. I gotta pee," Nick said gruffly.

"Get off at the next exit, Malcolm. We'll find someplace to eat and I can drive if you want."

"I'm fine driving. Actually, I'm kinda enjoying myself."

Savali smiled at him. "Glad you feel at home in my van."

Malcolm pulled off the freeway onto a road with a handful of gas stations and restaurants. "Any preferences?" he called out to the back.

"They can't see the choices back there, Malcolm. Just pick one. They're probably all the same."

Malcolm pulled into one and parked. "How do you open the goddam door, Savali?" Nick bellowed.

"Hold your horses. I'll come around and open it."

"Well, hurry up. I told you I gotta take a leak." She got out and opened the back. Nick hurried out and Finn was right behind him.

"I guess that's what I have to look forward to in my old age," Malcolm laughed.

"God, I hope not," Savali answered.

The restaurant was deserted except for a couple of field workers in sweat-stained cowboy hats, drinking beer and eating nachos. Malcolm and Savali sat down and waited for Finn and Nick to join them. A disinterested waitress brought some menus and two glasses of water. "Thanks. There will be two more coming." Malcolm smiled at the waitress who did not return the pleasantry. She sighed and shuffled back to the kitchen.

"Nice place you picked out, Malcolm," Nick said as he and Finn sat down. He lifted one of the glasses of water to take a drink, but stopped short. "I especially like the smell of the water."

"What do you have in cans or bottles?" Finn asked the waitress when she returned with two more glasses of water.

"Bud or Corona," she answered.

"Is the soda out of a machine or in cans?" Savali asked.

"Machine."

The foursome glanced at each other and said in unison, "Corona." They looked through the menu and ordered when the waitress returned with the beers.

"What time you figuring we'll get to San Francisco?" Finn asked Malcolm.

Malcolm looked at his phone and shrugged. "It'll still be around midnight if we get out of here in the next half hour."

"We're going to need to stop again, especially after this beer," Nick grunted.

"Even with a pit stop, we should make good time from now on."

"I don't want to get there too early anyway," Nick added. "I have to make sure the room is empty of visitors."

"I'll go up first and check," Savali offered.

"That's a stupid idea. Anthony knows you. If he's there he'll figure out I'm not far behind."

"Oh yeah. He knows you too, Malcolm, so it looks like Finn's gonna have to case the joint."

"I'm happy to help, but are you gonna clue me in on what the hell you're getting me into?" Finn asked.

Savali looked at Nick. "It's up to you to tell him, not me or Malcolm."

Nick didn't say anything, trying to decide what was enough to explain to Finn without disclosing his whole life story. He finally spoke. "My mother's in the hospital and I don't want to see any other members of my family."

Savali snorted. "You expect people to do shit for you and yet you can't be straight with them?"

Finn and Malcolm both started to speak at once, trying to diffuse the tension that was building in the air. "Shut up!" Nick bellowed at them. They stopped midsentence. "Okay. Finn, All the other members of my family are fucking drug dealers and I used to be one. I left the business and therefore my family is after me because they think I'm either going to tell the Feds or steal from them."

Finn didn't answer right away. Finally he said, "So why do you want to see your mother now?"

"She asked to see me before she dies."

"We never stop looking for love and approval from our parents, do we." Finn shook his head. "The world would be a better place if we could just let bygones be bygones."

Nick stared at Finn. Savali and Malcolm exchanged glances. And luckily the waitress brought the food so no one had to respond to Finn's comment. They finished their dinners in silence. "This wasn't that bad," Finn commented as he threw a couple of twenty-dollar bills on the table.

"You don't have to do that," Malcolm said.

"You guys pay for the gas. I'll take care of this," Finn answered. "C'mon Nick. Let's go drain our radiators before we hit the road."

"I guess we all should," Malcolm said as he followed Finn and Nick .He waited to see if Savali would follow them into the men's room or go the other way.

"I'll go fill up the tank across the street at the ARCO." Savali took the keys out of Malcolm's hand before he had a chance to protest. "Meet me over there."

Savali was nowhere to be found when the three of them got to the van. She came around from the side of the building after a couple of minutes. Malcolm peeked around the corner to study the order of the restroom doors, only to discover the ladies room had a sign taped on it saying it was out of order. She opened the back door for Finn and Nick. "You want to drive now or shall I?" Malcolm asked.

"I'll drive for a while. You can do the last stretch after the next pit stop. That way you can do the city driving."

"Okay," Malcolm said. He climbed into the passenger seat while Savali hopped into the driver's seat. She got the starter to catch on the first try and then mischievously popped the clutch.

"Jesus Christ!" Nick shouted. "And we thought Malcolm was bad!"

Savali shot a playful grin at Malcolm. "I just wanted to break the icy mood back there," she whispered to him.

"I think you did. Now the two of them can grouse about your driving instead of whether Nick's intentions are out of affection for his mother or out of his own neediness."

"Have you read any of Finn's books?"

"No. How many did he write?"

"A couple that I know of. One was his memoir called *Ode to Forgiveness*. He had a crappy childhood with a mother who didn't stand up against his alcoholic father who beat them both. He left Ireland and moved here and never saw her again. That's where he was coming from when he said that to Nick."

"I guess not every mother deserves enduring, unquestioned love."

"Life's just not that simple, Malcolm. Maybe you didn't have a complex relationship with your mother. It was terrible that she died when you were so young. But she was a good mother. You just really don't know what it's like."

"And you?"

"And me, what?"

"What kind of relationship did you have with your mother?"

"Complicated."

Malcolm nodded, not expecting any further details at this time. They fell into a comfortable silence as the van roared on over the dark, flat valley. The two old men fell fast asleep on the futon.

23

SAVALI PULLED OFF INTERSTATE 5 AT HARRIS RANCH. The reek from the mountains of manure at the feedlot just to the north failed to rouse the old men in the back, but Malcolm was already covering his face with his hand. Nick and Finn were fast asleep; they didn't even wake up as they drove past Harris Ranch.

"How do people stay at that motel and eat at that restaurant?" Malcolm gasped through his fingers.

"The premises stay sealed for their protection," Savali sniffed. "You only have to hold your breath when you're outside." She then turned her head and piped up, "Hey Shamu and Al Capone, time for your pit stop!"

There was a stirring and grumbling in back that suddenly broke off into choking. "Jesus Christ! What's that disgusting smell?" Nick snapped. "Did someone crap in their pants?"

"No. That's just cattle in purgatory. You two get out and do your thing, so we can get the hell out of here." She got out of the van and opened the back door. The wall of fumes momentarily stunned Nick and Finn, but they eventually hobbled off to an adjacent Minimart. "You coming Mata Hari?" she asked Malcolm.

"Mata Hari?" he asked as he got out of the passenger side.

"I don't know. I got tired of calling you James Bond. Wasn't that some famous spy?"

"Yeah, but . . . oh never mind." He walked next to Savali, eager to see which restroom she entered. But again, his hopes were thwarted when he saw one door plastered with an out of order sign and Finn waiting outside the other.

"Maybe the shit smell is from the lack of plumbing," Finn snorted.

Malcolm grinned. "Anybody want a drink or a snack while we wait?"

"Whiskey could make the smell bearable," Finn mused.

"Probably nothing but beer here."

"Forget it. I'll wait until we get to the city."

Nick came out and Finn went in. Malcolm went to the cash register with a bag of peanuts. Savali, meanwhile, was nowhere to be seen. The three men used the bathroom and went back to the van. Nick tried the door but it was locked. "Where the hell is Savali?" Nick asked.

"I don't know. I'll go back inside and look." Malcolm returned to the Minimart and when he came out, he saw Savali exiting the van, dressed in a tailored, button-down man's shirt and slacks.

"Why did you change your clothes?" Nick asked.

Savali shrugged. "Felt like it. You drive, Malcolm." She handed him the keys. Everyone scrambled into their respective seats and Malcolm started the van without incident. He pushed the column shift up towards him, backed the van out of the greasy parking spot, and dropped the lever down to first. The van rumbled away and with a deft shift up, he left the Minimart behind and entered the on-ramp. "I think you might drive my van better than I do," Savali murmured.

Malcolm smiled a little, but not at her. "Got to treat her like you want to be treated," he replied simply.

They drove in silence for a while. Savali closed her eyes and Malcolm glanced at her, trying to determine if she was asleep or simply meditative. When her mouth opened slightly, and her breathing became more regular, he decided she was sleeping. Whistles, puffs and low moans coming from the back reported that Finn and Nick had gone back to sleep, as well. Great. They'll all be rested and he'll be exhausted while they whittle the night away. Maybe he could just crash on Finn's friend's sofa. He wouldn't put it past Savali to have some crazy things she wanted to do in San Francisco in the middle of the night. Well, she could do them herself. Anyway, maybe that's why she dressed as a man now: to ward off any men. Or maybe it was because she wanted to attract the gay contingent. Malcolm killed a couple of hours trying to unravel the mystery that was Savali.

The passengers all awoke when Malcolm fumbled for his wallet as he approached the Bay Bridge Toll Plaza. "You need the toll?" Savali asked as she reached into her own pocket.

"Yeah, I might dump us into the bay trying to get my wallet out." She handed him a ten. He gave it to the toll taker and gave the change back to Savali. "One of the nice things about Los Angeles is no toll."

"Weather's better too," Savali replied.

"Are we here? What time is it?" Nick asked. His voice was shaky and taut.

"Just going over the bridge. Hey, I never asked what hospital your mother is in."

"That one named after that Facebook guy."

"What? Mark Zuckerberg?"

"Yeah, that's it."

"I didn't know he donated a bunch of money to a hospital. But that still doesn't tell me where it is?"

"Hold on," Savali said as she looked at her phone. "San Francisco General?"

"No. The other one, the one connected to the university," Nick answered.

"UCSF? Well, that's not the same place as San Francisco General and that's the one named after Zuckerberg. So which one is it?"

"Oh for Christ's sake. Let me look again." Nick took out a piece of paper from his pocket. "Oh, not the Zuckerberg one. They're connected and that's the number I called first. It's the UCSF one."

"And where's that?" Malcolm asked.

"Keep your pants on," Savali answered as she looked up the map on her phone. "At least for now." She winked at Malcolm who grinned and shook his head. "Okay. Get off here at Duboce and then go left on Market." She continued guiding Malcolm through the streets of San Francisco, arriving at the hospital about twenty minutes later.

Malcolm stopped the van. "Here we are, Nick. It's about twelve thirty. Shall we send Finn up first to see if the coast is clear?"

"How am I going to get into the room when visiting hours have been over for hours?" Finn asked.

"Ask for Lloyd. He's the night nurse who's waiting for me." Nick almost whispered.

"Yeah, brilliant idea. I say I'm you and then how do you get in?"

"Just say you're another brother of Anthony's." Savali chimed in.

"Oh, now I'm just an Italian leprechaun."

"For God's sake, Finn," Savali snapped. "No one cares that much. The lady's dying. What can happen to her?"

"Oh I'll go!" Nick suddenly shouted. "Just open this goddam door!"

Savali got out and opened the back of the van. "Want us to wait in the waiting room?"

"Just go. I have that phone Malcolm got me. I'll call you when I'm ready."

Malcolm and Savali looked at each other, unsure if this was the wisest plan. "I don't know, Nick." Malcolm finally said. "I still think it would be better for Finn to check out that no one is there, first."

"Why don't you call that Lloyd fellow at the nurse's station and see if the coast is clear?" Finn suggested.

"Yeah!" Malcolm and Savali said in unison.

Nick looked up the number and called. "I'm calling about Francesca Balducci. Is Lloyd there?" He was quiet for some time as the sound of distorted music drifted from his phone. "Yeah, hey Lloyd. Is anyone else there? Okay, thanks." He hung up. "The coast is clear. I'll call you." He got out of the van and walked toward the entrance, often looking side to side and behind himself. The three others watched him enter the building.

"Where to, Finn?" Malcolm asked.

"Go back to Stanyan and take a left." Finn looked at a piece of paper he had taken from his pocket and read off the directions. After a couple of mistaken turns due to Finn's inability to read his own handwriting, they finally pulled up in front of a small, pink stucco house perched high above the street.

"This is it."

"What do you want to do, Malcolm?" Savali asked. "Do you want to stay here with Finn? I was going to go to a couple of clubs and check them out."

"I don't know. I thought we were going to stay here with Finn's friend."

"Whatever you want. I'm just giving you the option."

"Can you open this goddam door while you're making this earth-shattering decision?"

"I see you haven't mellowed out completely in your old age," Savali replied.

Savali got out of the passenger seat and opened the door. Malcolm got out with her, still unsure whether or not he wanted to go with her. What clubs was she talking about? Gay ones? Is that why she dressed back up as a man? Or did she want to go trolling for women? He wanted to go with her, if it would just be the two of them going out. "So what's your plan?" she asked.

"I think I'll stay here with Finn. I'm really tired from all the driving. Make sure you keep your phone on and check it often. It'll be loud in those places so you won't hear it."

"Yes, Mommy! Is Nick going to call you or me?"

"Does he know your number?"

"Probably not. Text me after you've heard from him. I'll go pick him up first."

"Are you okay to drive in the city?"

Savali shook her head and grinned at Malcolm. "I've managed many years driving all over the place without you."

"Well, earlier you said you didn't like driving in the city."

"It doesn't mean I can't. I just prefer not to if I have the option."

"Okay." He wasn't sure whether to tell her to have fun. He didn't really want her to.

Before he had to choose whether or not to say it, Finn piped up. "Jesus, you two are ridiculous! It's freezing out here! I'm going in." Finn started climbing the stairs edged with neatly tended flowers.

Malcolm called out. "I'm coming." He handed the keys to Savali and ran after Finn, catching up to him just as he got to the front door and rang the bell.

The door opened and a black man reached out and grabbed Finn in a bear hug. "Finn!" They hugged while Malcolm stood by, trying to figure out why that voice sounded familiar. Finn's wild mane of white hair mostly obscured his friend's face.

They finally pulled apart and Finn said, "This is Malcolm. Malcolm, this is Jed." Both their jaws dropped and before either one spoke, Malcolm's eyes filled with tears and Jed wrapped his arms around him.

24

MALCOLM DIDN'T LET GO OF JED FOR A COUPLE OF MINUTES. He didn't want Finn to know he was crying, but Jed felt the quivering of his body. He held onto him tightly, knowing that Malcolm might be embarrassed. Finn hadn't known that they knew each other, but as he stood there watching them hug, he put the pieces together. They must have met in Venice when Jed lived there. Malcolm must have been just a kid then.

They finally let go of one another and went inside. "Well, if you wanted to surprise me, you certainly did the job!" Jed said as he brought them into the living room.

"I had no idea," Malcolm murmured.

"Finn didn't tell you?"

"He never said your name. Just that it was a friend."

Jed turned to Finn. "Don't you remember that I knew a kid on the boardwalk?"

"Yeah, but I never knew his name," Finn answered.

"Kate never told you?" Jed asked. "Your daughter was his teacher when she taught at Venice High. You remember when Ruby died and Kate put her in the columbarium? She told me when she was here then that she had run into Malcolm working at the homeless resource table on the boardwalk."

"Miss McGee is Finn's daughter?" Malcolm asked.

"You didn't know all that?"

"I guess none of us put two and two together. Hey Jed, remember when you came to my high school when I got that award? You and Miss McGee met then. You and Finn already knew each other?" Malcolm asked.

"This is getting way too confusing for my old brain!" Finn shook his head.

"I can explain it all," Jed said. "But first, what can I get you? Are you still drinking Jameson's, Finn?"

"If you have some."

"I bought a bottle just for you," Jed smiled.

"That's kind of you."

"How about you Malcolm?"

"A beer would be fine."

Jed went into the kitchen and returned with a glass of whiskey and two beers. He sat down. "Monica wanted me to wake her up unless you would still be here in the morning. She wants to meet you."

"We don't know how long we're staying. We have to wait for Nick to call when he's ready and then Savali will pick him up and they'll both come here to pick us up. We just don't know when that'll be."

"Well, I'll let her sleep and wake her after a while."

"So, do we want to hear the story of Jed and Malcolm and rehash the past, or talk about the present?" Finn asked.

Jed shook his head. "Still working on that. Writing a book about it didn't get you any closer to letting the past go?"

"Absolutely. I did let it go. I am no longer a prisoner to it. I, for one, don't need to know the backstory of the two of you. How about you?"

"Yep, me too. I've got too many good things happening now."

"Like Monica?" Malcolm finally joined in the conversation. "She's your . . .?"

Jed smiled broadly. "My wife."

"You're kidding!" Finn and Malcolm chorused in unison.

"Is it that shocking that I could find a woman who likes me enough to marry me?" Jed teased.

"It's not that. You were just such a loner. I can't imagine you sharing your life with someone."

"I'm happy for you, Jed," Malcolm said quietly.

"How about you? Anyone special in your life, Malcolm?"

Jed glanced at Finn, hoping he wouldn't make some wisecrack about Savali. "No," he answered quickly. Finn didn't say a word. He just gave Malcolm a knowing, half smile.

The three men talked for a couple of hours, sharing the last several years of their lives. The whiskey got to Finn and he fell asleep in his chair. Jed's had lived so many years with inconsistent sleep patterns, that he was barely affected by the fact that it was the middle of the night. Malcolm was young enough to just push his tiredness aside. His adrenaline was high, anyway, from seeing Jed again. These two continued the conversation until the streetlight outside the window went out. "It's been a long time since I pulled an all-nighter," Jed smiled.

"I'm sorry. You didn't have to stay up for me."

"Are you kidding, Malcolm? I wouldn't have wanted to miss a minute of time with you. I've thought about you so often, wondering what happened to you. And now, I'm so proud of what you've become. Miss Ruthie did a wonderful job."

"I've thought about you, too. I never thought I'd see you again. I didn't know what happened to you. I didn't know where you had gone or why."

"Well, it doesn't matter now. Here we are. And we will stay in touch."

At that moment Malcolm's cell phone rang. He answered, "Nick? Oh, Savali. No, I haven't heard from him yet. You're probably right. You want to pick us up first? Okay. See you in a few." He hung up. "Maybe you should go wake Monica so we can meet her. I'll rouse sleeping beauty over here." Jed went to the bedroom to get Monica. "Hey Finn, we need to go."

Finn opened his eyes. "Gotta use the bathroom." He got up and stumbled into the hall and after opening the linen closet, found the right door.

The doorbell rang and Malcolm looked out the window to see Savali standing there. He answered the door before Jed could. "How'd you get here so fast?"

"I was actually just down the street when I called." Savali entered the living room just as Monica, Finn and Jed did. The introductions were made and niceties said, Monica's while stifling a yawn. Jed and Savali vaguely remembered each other from their boardwalk days.

"So, why do you think Nick hasn't called?" Finn asked.

Savali shrugged. "I'm a little concerned. I didn't think he'd last this long in the hospital room."

Monica and Jed exchanged glances. "Nick's on the run from his gangster family," Finn explained.

Savali shot Malcolm a look of alarm. "No worries, Savali. Jed and Monica are cool."

"So why is he at the hospital?" Monica asked.

"His mother's dying. He wanted to see her," Finn answered.

"Well, we'd better get there before visiting hours start."

"Before visiting hours start? Strange time to visit one's mother in the hospital," Monica commented.

"It's complicated," Malcolm smiled. "Sorry that we can't explain more right now." Malcolm turned to Jed. "You have my number now and I have yours."

"We'll stay in touch," Monica promised. They all hugged goodbye and Savali, Finn and Malcolm got into the van and drove off.

25

THEY DROVE IN SILENCE, LOST IN THEIR OWN FEARS OF WHAT MIGHT HAVE HAPPENED TO NICK. The sun was in their eyes by the time they arrived at the hospital parking lot. The dazzle added to their daze over the situation, and no one bothered to squint at their phones for the time or messages. Malcolm turned to Savali. "Well, how do you want to handle this?"

"Why are you asking me?"

"I guess I was just starting the discussion. Any thoughts?"

"I suppose we go inside the hospital and go to Nick's mother's room and see if he's there."

"All of us?"

"Why not? Wait a minute . . . are you afraid of Nick's family?"

"Maybe . . . a little."

"There's safety in numbers."

"Well, I—"

"Fine, Caspar Milquetoast. I'll go."

"Maybe you should put a dress on. They wouldn't hurt a woman."

Savali laughed. "Yeah, especially one in a leather skirt and kick ass boots." She went to the back of the van, only to encounter a minor problem alongside her discarded skirt and boots. "Hey Finn, would you mind going into the front with Malcolm?"

"C'mon Finn," Malcolm said. "We'll wait outside."

Savali emerged from the van a few minutes later, looking like dynamite. Even Finn raised his eyebrows with admiration. "Okay guys. If I don't come out in fifteen minutes, call the cops! I may have to file a report about a boot missing in action." She laughed and strode off.

Finn and Malcolm got back in the van. This time Finn sat in the passenger seat. "Well, that was a surprise. I didn't know you were the Malcolm both Jed and Kate had spoken of years ago. Small world."

"What a treat for me to spend time with Jed. I've thought about him so much. Thanks."

"Thank serendipity, not me. Jed wasn't exactly sorry to see you, either."

"He saved my life when I was a kid."

"Mine too, Malcolm. And many others, I'm sure. So tell me, what's your relationship to Savali?"

Malcolm stiffened. He was inclined to tell him it was none of his business, but eventually just answered truthfully. "I don't know."

Finn cocked his head and furrowed his brow. "You don't know?"

"Have you asked Savali the same question?"

"No. I wouldn't get a straight answer from Savali like I would from you."

"Well, that's the truth. I don't know. We work together and we're friends."

"Then you do know."

Malcolm looked at Finn to see if his face showed any signs that he was kidding. It was hard to tell. "Okay. Then that's the extent of our relationship."

Finn smiled at him. "If you say so."

"Has it been fifteen minutes?"

"I thought Savali was kidding. She was serious?"

"I don't know. But maybe we need to check. The way Nick talked about his brother and his family . . ."

"I doubt they would hurt Savali in a hospital."

"I'll text her." Malcolm took out his phone and texted her. There was no immediate response, so Malcolm decided to call her, thinking maybe she didn't hear the text. But before he finished dialing, Savali appeared at the entrance to the hospital, walking toward the van.

She came to the driver's side and Malcolm opened the window. She looked worried. "He left hours ago, according to the nurse." She looked into Malcolm's eyes. "With his brother."

"Shit!" Malcolm said. "What should we do?"

"What can we do?"

"Call him, for starters."

"I did. The phone's not working."

"Did you ask his mother anything?" Finn asked.

"Apparently, I don't look like family."

"Huh?"

"The nurse wouldn't tell me."

"Did he spend any time with her before his brother appeared?" Malcolm asked.

"He was only there a few minutes before Anthony returned. I got that much out of the nurse, anyway. I'm guessing he waited somewhere, watching for Nick."

"Oh man. What are we going to do? We can't go to the police because it might get Nick in trouble too."

"I think all we can do is wait for him to contact us," Savali sighed.

"It might be too late."

"You two kids really think you are equipped to deal with gangsters?" Finn laughed bitterly. "They have guns, money and plenty of scum working for them who aren't afraid to do whatever it takes to get what they want. Nick made his own bed, as the saying goes. You two have done more than enough to help him. If you're not going to call the police, there is nothing else to do."

Malcolm and Savali looked at each other and then at the hospital entrance. She sighed and said, "All this makes me very tired. I need to lie down in the back." Savali walked around the van, opened the back door, and threw herself on the futon.

Finn turned away from the view of her leather skirt riding high on her hips. "So, where to now, chauffeur Malcolm?"

"I have no idea. I hate to leave San Francisco now. What if Nick needs us?"

Finn sighed his disapproval. "Well, you could buy us some time by finding us something to eat." He turned toward the back. "Savali? Are you hungry or do you just want to sleep?"

She was already half unconscious. "Well, that Mexican food is long gone," she mumbled into the futon. "Maybe that's what's wrong with me."

"I wonder what's nearby . . ."

"The hospital cafeteria?" Malcolm asked.

"Seriously?" Finn made a face. "Okay. I get it. You don't want to leave the area. Fine. How bad could it be? Never mind. It doesn't matter. Let's go." They piled out of the van and walked back toward the hospital.

They chose a few light items from the lackluster selection in the cafeteria and ate in silence. Malcolm and Savali checked their phones often, afraid they were missing a text or call. Not that they knew what they were expecting to happen. Everyone was thinking the worst, but no one said a word.

Finally Finn sighed. "Are we going to sit in this place until lunchtime?"

Savali exploded. "What the hell are we supposed to do, Finn? Go about our business like nothing's happened?"

"I'm sorry, Savali. But I doubt he's here in the hospital so we really don't need to be staying here."

"Finn's right," Malcolm said. "They've probably taken him somewhere else."

"Yeah, but Anthony should be coming back here and that's the only way we're going to find Nick."

"But if Anthony has Nick, the deed is done," Finn retorted. "Nick took the bait. It was never about their mother. There is no reason for anyone to come back here."

"Just wait and see." Malcolm patted Finn's arm. "We have to give it a chance."

"Well, then we should be up in that old lady's room, not here."

Malcolm and Savali looked at each other, sheepishly. They got up. "What's the room number?" Malcolm asked.

"Follow me," Savali answered. They filed out the door with Savali in the lead.

They arrived at the door to Nick's mother's room and peered inside. No one was in there. Various machines were hooked up to her and beeped or breathed life into her body.

A nurse approached them suspiciously. "Have you signed in? I don't recall seeing you here before." She looked Savali up and down and then turned her gaze to Malcolm. "Immediate family only, you know."

"Uh . . ." Malcolm fumbled for an excuse.

"If you have any business being here, you can go to the waiting room at the end of the hall," the nurse ordered with a wave of her hand. She gave Savali a final, appraising once over. "The family is usually here by now."

"Okay, thanks," Malcolm smiled sheepishly.

They sat for about an hour, thumbing through magazines and checking their phones for voice mail and texts. Malcolm and Savali were too distracted to indulge in anything else on their phones, and Finn never developed the habit. Finn got up to use the bathroom and when he returned, the waiting room was empty. He looked down the hall and saw a group of hospital personnel scurrying around, in and out of the room. Malcolm and Savali were standing well aside in the hall, watching the commotion. Finn approached them. "What's going on?"

"Code blue," Malcolm answered.

"She died?"

"I don't think so. That's why they're all in there."

"But no family members?"

"Not yet."

Finn nodded, and they stood silently watching the ritualistic pandemonium. Finally, the group filed out of the room. They watched the faces of the people leaving, trying to decipher the outcome, but they couldn't tell. Savali waited until the hall was clear and then opened the door and peeked inside. "The sheet's pulled over her head," she said.

"Well, a family member will have to be here soon, then," Finn added.

"At least Nick got to see her before she died," Malcolm asserted.

"But she didn't know," Savali sighed.

"They know, even when they're in a coma," Malcolm answered. He and Finn glanced at each other, somehow knowing that the other person had been in that situation before with a loved one.

They congregated back at the van, all three of them getting in the back, leaving the door open. Finn and Savali sat on the futon while Malcolm sat on the floor. "What now?" Finn asked.

"We should wait and see if Nick comes back," Savali answered.

"Does a member of the family have to come and identify the body?" Malcolm asked.

"The woman died here. Why do they need someone to identify the body? They already know who she was." Savali snapped.

"Maybe not, but they have to come and get the woman's belongings," Finn said.

Malcolm crawled out of the van. "I think we need to talk to someone and find out what's going on."

"Fine, but who do we talk to?" Savali asked as she followed him out. Finn was close behind.

"Let' see what we can find out." The three walked back to the hospital and back to the hallway outside Francesca's room.

Malcolm walked down the hall, peeking into rooms until he finally found an orderly inside one of them. He returned momentarily and shrugged. "We've been waiting for nothing. "You were right. No one needs to identify the body. They'll be sending it to a funeral home as soon as they find out which one. That's where we need to go."

"Well, doesn't someone need to come and get her things?" asked Savali.

"And what would a dying woman have in her room?" snorted Finn. "A tiara and a ball gown?"

Malcolm ignored him. "Maybe they just send them on to the funeral home."

"So how do we find out which funeral home?"

"The person I talked to said we can't get that information unless we're family."

"Shit. So who can we ask?"

"Maybe the nurse who Nick had talked to. Do you remember his name?" Malcolm asked.

"Was it Todd? No, wait. It ended in D; that I remember. Chad? No, that wasn't it. Let me think." Savali stared at the floor. "Lloyd!"

"Yeah," Malcolm agreed. "That was it. Let's see if he's here." The three traipsed off to the nurse's station and found out that Lloyd would be coming to work at three.

"Well, we can have lunch then," Finn said. "A real lunch in a real restaurant, preferably one that serves liquor." They found a place a couple of blocks away. When they sat down and ordered their food, Savali and Malcolm were finally able to relax enough to realize that they were exhausted. Finn had slept last night, but neither Savali nor Malcolm had shut their eyes at all. They were barely able to stay awake during the meal, but they were also hungry. "You two go to the van and take a nap. I'll stay here and wake you up at three."

"Great idea," Malcolm said as he threw some cash onto the table. He and Savali walked back to the van, and he was so tired that he didn't even question the fact that they would be sleeping next to each other on a full-size futon. Their bodies touched, but it felt natural and comfortable, even when Savali nestled into Malcolm's outstretched arm. They were deep in slumber before either of them considered anything other than sleep.

26

MALCOLM AND SAVALI WOKE WITH A START WHEN THEY HEARD FINN POUNDING ON THE BACK DOOR TO THE VAN. "It's almost four," Finn yelled.

"Oh crap!" Savali said as she jumped off the futon.

"Lloyd's not going anywhere," Malcolm mumbled as he rubbed his eyes. "His shift just started an hour ago."

"Yeah, I guess. Jeez, I could sure use a bathroom!" Savali fumbled through a box and found a toothbrush and toothpaste. "Do you need a toothbrush?"

"I have one." Malcolm produced one from his pants pocket.

"You certainly are resourceful." She winked.

Finn opened the door. "Sure hope you two are decent." Savali laughed. Malcolm looked mortified. "Just joking, Malcolm."

The three traipsed back inside the hospital, looking for restrooms. "Now you have a taste of what it's like living in a van," Savali said darkly.

"You mean always looking for the closest bathroom?" Malcolm responded.

"Yeah, and trying to fall asleep midst slamming car doors as you suffocate from gas vapors. Not to mention the fights and the drunks."

"I guess there's something to be said for your own bed in your own house."

"Beats a cardboard box, anyway." When they got outside the doors leading to the restrooms, Malcolm paused, wanting to see which one Savali chose. She stopped outside the women's and smiled at Malcolm. "I'll use this one today. I think I'm dressed for the occasion."

They got to the nurse's station and asked for Lloyd. He was with a patient, so they stood there and waited. The unit clerk asked them to go to the atrium, but they ignored her. He finally appeared and Savali went up to him before he reached the station. "How ya doin', Lloyd. We were wondering if you could help us."

"What do you need?" Lloyd asked.

"Where they brought Francesca Balducci's body. I mean, what funeral home."

"Can't you just ask at the mortuary downstairs?"

"They wouldn't tell us. We're not family."

"They'll have it in the obituary won't they? So people can come to the funeral?"

"C'mon, Lloyd. Just find out for us, will you? We aren't planning to steal the body. We can't go to the funeral. We need to leave and get back to Los Angeles."

"I don't know . . . I don't want to get into trouble . . ."

"We're not going to tell anyone. Hold on." She went back to Malcolm. "You got a twenty on you?"

"Twenty? How about ten?" Malcolm reached into his wallet and handed Savali a ten.

She rolled her eyes but took it and turned to hand it to Lloyd. "Okay?" Lloyd grimaced but went back to the unit desk and got on the phone. He returned and silently handed Savali a piece of paper. "Thanks," she said, but he turned abruptly and walked down the hall without saying a word.

The three filed out of the hospital for the last time. They took their seats in the van,

Malcolm driving, Savali navigating, and Finn trying to stay upright on the futon in the back. "Where am I going?" Malcolm asked.

"Back toward Jed's. The funeral home is on Geary, but not downtown. Go toward the ocean."

"Has anyone figured out what exactly we're going to do once we get there?" Finn called from the back. Savali and Malcolm looked to each other for an answer. Neither spoke, however. The silence was interrupted by Finn's sigh. "That's what I thought."

They drove down Geary, lost in their own thoughts. "What number on Geary?" Malcolm finally said.

"I don't know. It's coming up, though. It's near Arguello. There it is." Savali pointed to a nondescript cement building. Malcolm parked in the lot. They piled out of the van and went inside. The lobby had lots of red velvet on the walls, lit by a myriad of crystal chandeliers. There was a Victorian settee and chairs, and an ornate coffee table, covered with bound catalogs extolling the virtues of various coffins and urns.

"Good afternoon. May I help you?" A young man who didn't look old enough to vote, approached them. He was dressed in a black suit that was too big for his skinny frame.

"We're here for Francesca Balducci," Savali interjected before Malcolm had a chance to open his mouth.

"Yes, I believe she was just brought in this morning." He looked at them, one at a time. "Are you, um, the family?"

Again Savali answered quickly, "Yes."

The young man's expression turned from bright and compassionate to quizzical and doubting. Finn, meanwhile, broke out in loud guffaws. "Sure we are. Don't we three look like Italian stallions! I'd say it's more like the Village People!"

Malcolm tried to suppress his own laughter as he looked at the man with the white mane and Irish brogue, the brown-skinned South Pacific Islander and his own black skin. "We are close friends. We need to speak with her sons and we were hoping we'd catch them here," Malcolm managed to say with a straight face.

"I see. Well, no family member has come yet."

"Have they called? Do you know when they're coming?" Savali asked.

"Not as yet. They don't usually call. They just come." The young man was starting to soften, so Savali figured she'd use her feminine wiles. "Maybe we should call them," she said airily. Then she focused a coquettish smile on the young man. "I've left their number at home. It's been so long since I talked to them. Do you have it?"

It worked. Nothing like a young man's libido getting stroked. And Savali was so good at it. "Sure. Just a minute and I'll get it." He grinned foolishly at her and went into the office.

"Your skills remain undiminished," murmured Finn.

"Thanks, Finn." Savali looked over at Malcolm for further compliments, but he just beamed at her.

The young man returned with a scrap of paper and handed it to Savali. "Would you like to use the office phone?" he said.

"Oh that's sweet of you, but we'll call from the car. What's your name?" Savali batted her eyelashes.

Malcolm and Finn groaned softly in unison, but the young man didn't catch on at all. "Wayne." He swallowed, his Adam's apple bobbing.

"What a nice name. Maybe I'll see you later," she said as she brushed her hand over his. Finn and Malcolm faked somber expressions lest they burst out laughing until they all exited the funeral parlor cum bordello.

"Good lord, Savali," Finn snorted when they got outside. "That poor boy is going to be glued to his shorts after that display."

"Hey, it got us what we wanted. If you got it, flaunt it." She had posed studiously over the slip of paper in her hand as she spoke and now started dialing.

"Hold it," Malcolm said. "What are you going to say when they answer?"

"I'm going to ask for Anthony. And then ask him where Nick is. It's pretty straightforward. Did you have another idea?"

"Nope." Malcolm watched Savali dial. Finn, meanwhile, started playing solitaire with a deck of cards.

"Hello? Is Anthony there? Oh. Do you have his number? This is a friend from Los Angeles. I'd rather not. Well, what about Dominick? Is he there?" She looked at Malcolm and shrugged. "Oh. Okay. Do you know when they'll be at the funeral home? Okay, okay. I get it. Fine. Thanks for nothing." She hung up. "Fucking asshole."

"Savali. These are drug dealers. Did you really think they were going to give out information to someone who wasn't even willing to say her name?"

"Well, I am a little more persuasive in person."

Malcolm just shook his head. "You're too much. At any rate, what's next? We need to get back to Venice, you know. We have jobs."

"We can't just leave Nick here, wherever the hell he is."

"Did it ever dawn on you that maybe Nick chose not to call?" Finn suggested. "Maybe he wanted to disappear on his own?"

Savali and Malcolm looked at each other. "We didn't even think of that," Malcolm said.

"I guess that's possible, but he left with Anthony, remember?" Savali replied.

"It's more than possible," Finn said. "It's probable."

"Let's just get out of here before rush hour gets unbearable," Malcolm added.

"Too late for that, but okay." Malcolm started the van and pulled away from the curb as Savali put her phone away and Finn settled in for another nap.

They pulled up in front of Finn's daughter's apartment building in Westwood a bit after one in the morning. They had stopped twice: once for dinner and once more for gas and a pit stop. Finn scampered out of the van quickly. He had not wanted to ask them to stop one more time. "I'll see you both tomorrow. Kate and her husband are going to help me move some stuff in."

"Cool. I'd like to see them again."

"Yeah, she's looking forward to seeing you too. Did you know she was in the Peace Corps these last two years?"

"No, I didn't. Wow. Where was she?"

"Can we have this little discussion tomorrow? I, uh, need to get upstairs."

Savali laughed. "Needed another pit stop did you?"

"Oh shut up."

Savali got out and opened the back door for Finn and then opened the door to the driver's side. "Scoot over. I'll drive now and drop you off at your house."

Malcolm got into the passenger seat, but debated about how to respond. Did she expect him to offer to have her stay with him? Did he want her to? Well, she could sleep in Nick's room since he wasn't there. Then there wouldn't be much weird stuff to worry about. He really needed to figure this whole situation out. "Why don't you stay at my house? You could sleep in Nick's room."

She didn't say anything until she stopped at a red light, and then presented herself by turning her whole body toward him. "Sure. I'd like to stay at your house." She took a breath, but before she could say anymore, the light turned green and the car behind her honked. She shifted her body in defeat and popped the clutch. They didn't speak the entire way to Malcolm's. She parked and they got out, still without saying a word.

Malcolm took out his key and opened the door. He turned on a light in the living room. "I'm exhausted. Do you need anything?" he asked.

Savali looked him over and sighed. "Not right now."

Malcolm shivered but turned away from his desire. "Good night."

Savali watched him walk down the hall. When he was finished in the bathroom, she went in, found herself a towel, and took a long, hot shower. After drying off, she studied herself in the mirror. She ran a hand down her cheek, over her jaw and down her neck, checking for stubble. Satisfied with her inspection, she wrapped the towel around herself and started down the hall. She hesitated at Malcolm's door, adjusting the towel into an alluring fashion. And then she sighed again and went on to Nick's room.

27

MALCOLM WOKE UP AND CHECKED HIS PHONE. It was only eight, plenty of time to get to work. He threw on a pair of basketball shorts and went to the bathroom to shower. He stopped at the door to Nick's room and listened, wondering if Savali was awake. She usually got to work earlier than him and liked to go to Muscle Beach or the gym first. He didn't hear anything but decided to shower before waking her. He continued down the hall to the bathroom but found that door closed. Hmm, there were advantages to living alone in a one-bathroom house. He went on to the kitchen to start the coffee pot instead. He was trying to decide if he should just go pee outside in the back yard when Savali appeared in workout clothes.

"Good morning." Malcolm half danced. "I'll be right back!" He scurried off to the bathroom. When he returned, Savali was not there. He peeked out the living room window and the van was also gone. This was not the kind of weirdness he had expected. He distracted himself by showering, dressing, pouring a cup of coffee and taking it to his computer.

He spent the next half hour Googling the San Francisco newspapers, looking for Francesca's obituary. He had thought that maybe they should go back for the funeral so they could talk to Anthony. He couldn't imagine that Nick's own family would have hurt him. Maybe Finn was right and Nick left on his own. But then, if he had been hiding, he obviously wouldn't go to his mother's funeral. And if Anthony had kidnapped him, he certainly wasn't going to tell Malcolm where he was. He was just going to have to leave this alone and hope that Nick would contact them.

He got to Moss House and searched for Savali in the office, but she wasn't there. He went back to the community room to set up for Writer's Workshop and found George and Homer sitting on the sofa, reading the paper. "Good Morning," Malcolm said as he entered.

"Hey, Malcolm. How was your trip?" Homer asked.

"Good, thanks. Quick. How was everything here? Did the classes go well?"

"Yeah. Jose and I did the Music on Tuesday and George gave us some boxing instruction instead of Savali's Yoga and Pilates."

Malcolm grinned at George. "You did?" George grunted. "Did the boxing help, Homer?"

"Yes. And I tried Violet's line dancing too. It was all good."

"It helped the tremors?"

"Some."

"Did you get a new phone?"

"George drove me to the phone store. I've been waiting for you to get back to teach me how to use it."

"Let's do that this afternoon after the writing class." Malcolm went back to setting up the room. The writers started sauntering in and he went back to the office, but still no Savali.

He returned to the community room and stood at the doorway, watching everyone get settled with their notebooks and pens. A couple of people even had laptops and iPads. Everyone greeted Malcolm as if he had been gone for weeks, rather than a couple of days. The workshop leaders changed each week. Luckily there were a few retired teachers with the classroom management skills needed to deal with this sometimes unruly group. Older people could be as difficult to deal with as little kids. Today the leader was an ex-fifth grade teacher named Jean. She had brought a prompt to start the workshop. They wrote quickly without worrying about grammar and spelling, just writing from the heart. "Did you bring paper, Malcolm?" Jean asked.

"No. Can I borrow some?" He was inundated with people tearing out sheets of paper and handing them to him. He took a couple of pieces and a pen and settled into a seat at the table. The prompt was especially appropriate: "Write about a time when you had to make a choice about something and felt unable to decide what to do."

He had filled up both sides of the two pages quickly and had more to write when Jean called out that time was up. She asked if anyone wanted to share. It wasn't mandatory, and Malcolm definitely wasn't ready to share his. Especially since most of it was stuff he didn't want these people to know. He wrote about his own career challenges, trying to decide what direction he should go. He also wrote about Nick's disappearance and how sometimes there just weren't any good choices. And then he wrote about his feelings for Savali and how there were sometimes clear choices, but his fears got in the way.

The time went quickly. A few people read their prompts aloud, but these were never critiqued so it only took twenty minutes or so. Then the real workshop began where people shared what they were working on. The comments could be pretty brutal but were meant to be constructive, so the writers welcomed the criticism. Malcolm listened for a while, but he kept jumping up to check whether Savali had arrived.

At noon, when the workshop broke up, she still hadn't appeared. He asked Jose if he'd heard from her and his response was that Malcolm should be the person who knows. Jose was right, of course. She hadn't responded to his texts. He wished he had Finn's number, but he'd forgotten to get it. Well, Finn had said he and Ms. McGee, or Kate, would be here today, moving in some stuff. It's kind of weird that Savali goes missing right after Nick does.

Malcolm grabbed a burger on the boardwalk and brought it back to the community room. Homer was there, waiting for him with his new phone, so he put off eating his lunch while he helped Homer figure out texting. He also showed him how to access the

Internet on it, but it was too small for him to read.

"How was the writing class?" Homer asked.

"I enjoyed it," Malcolm answered. "Why didn't you come to that? Your story would be very interesting. You could write your memoir."

"I can't write or type, I'm afraid. The hand shakes too much."

Malcolm fiddled with Homer's phone for a minute and then showed it to him. "Look at this app. It's a recorder. You could speak into it and then I could transcribe it. There's even software that would do that. Maybe I can talk to Annabel and she could buy it for the Moss House. I'm sure there are plenty of others who would like to write their stories but aren't comfortable or fast on the computer."

"This phone is a recorder too? Wow. It does everything."

Malcolm laughed. "These smart phones are remarkable. Try recording something tonight and see how it works."

"Thanks, Malcolm. Jeez, this is great."

"Glad to help."

Homer left and Malcolm gobbled down his burger. Savali finally appeared just after two.

She nodded to Malcolm and then went into the office. She was dressed in a T-shirt and jeans and wore a baseball cap. She looked like a twelve year-old boy. He knew she was avoiding him, but he wasn't going to let her get away with it. He followed her into the office.

"What is it Malcolm? I have a lot of work to do after missing a couple of days."

"What's this attitude about?" Malcolm asked.

"What attitude?"

"Come on, Savali. You left the house this morning without a word, you're five hours late for work and you're barely acknowledging me. Is something wrong? Are you mad at me?"

Savali exhaled loudly and looked away from Malcolm. "No. I'm just busy."

"Where were you this morning?"

"I don't have to tell you."

"True, but I don't get it. Everything was fine and then, out of nowhere, you're acting . . . oh never mind." Malcolm started to walk out.

"Okay. Something is wrong."

Malcolm turned around. "What did I do?"

"It's not what you did, Malcolm. It's what you didn't do."

"What? I didn't work hard enough to find Nick? I would have done whatever it took if I'd had any idea what to do. We couldn't call the police and we weren't going to get anywhere with Anthony or any other member of his family."

Savali bit her lip and looked into Malcolm's eyes. "When are we going to talk about our relationship?"

"Uh, our relationship?" he stuttered.

"Yes."

"I don't know. What do you mean?"

"Oh, Malcolm! You know damn well what I mean."

Malcolm looked down at his shoes and breathed heavily. Why did she bring this up now? He had no idea how to answer her. But she was right. They needed to clarify what's going on. "This is very confusing for me. Okay? Yes. I'm attracted to you. But I'm not gay. So I don't really know what's going on. I don't know how to behave or what to do about it. Satisfied?"

Savali stood up slowly and walked to the door and shut it. Then she turned around and took Malcolm's face in her hands and kissed him. Malcolm resisted at first, but then he allowed himself to melt into a passionate kiss.

She took her lips away. "That's what you do about it."

Malcolm touched his lips and stared at her. He turned away and sat down in the empty office chair. He looked down at the papers on the desk and didn't speak. After a couple of minutes, he stood up and turned to Savali. "I'm leaving early. I need some time to myself right now before I go to the cafe. We can continue the conversation another time." He left.

"Okay," she whispered, smiling.

28

MALCOLM WAS THE FIRST SERVER OFF THAT NIGHT AND LEFT THE CAFE JUST AFTER NINE. He looked forward to being in his own house, his own bed, and without the presence of Savali and the two curmudgeons. He laughed. It sounded like the name of a band: Savali and The Curmudgeons. He picked up a six-pack and a salad at Whole Foods, relishing the idea of a meal for one that was both nutritious and indulgent. He then turned the corner of his street and noticed Savali's van. She was parked right in front of his house. His heart skipped a beat at the same time as the corners of his mouth turned down into a frown. That physical reaction perfectly exemplified how he felt. He was excited seeing Savali, but he really didn't want her company. He knew he would invite her in, but furthering their complicated relationship would do nothing right now to help him understand it.

Savali got out of the van when Malcolm got to his front door. "If you don't want me to come in, just say so, but you said you wanted to continue the conversation."

"Come in. Did you have dinner? I can share my salad if you haven't."

"That's okay. I ate. I'll just have one of those beers."

Malcolm got out a plate and a fork, opened two beers and sat down at the dining room table. Savali sat down across from him. She was dressed in her usual unisex costume: jeans and a T-shirt, but she did have make-up on. "I don't usually get home this early. You might have been waiting out there a long time."

She grinned. "I live in my van, Malcolm. If you hadn't invited me in, I would have just stayed parked here and gone to sleep."

"Oh, yeah." He took a few bites of food and Savali stayed quiet. She had made her move and showed how she felt. It was up to Malcolm to go next. He shrugged. "I guess I don't know what to say."

"How about just say what you feel."

"But that's just it. I don't know how I feel."

"Yes you do. You just don't want to face it."

Malcolm didn't reply. He finished his salad and the beer and then brought his plate into the kitchen. He returned with two more beers. He sat down and sighed. "Okay. I like you and I'm attracted to you. But I'm straight and you're . . ."

Savali's attention glazed over as she waited to see how he would finish that sentence. He looked down at his beer and twirled the bottle around in his hands. "Do you want me to finish the sentence for you?" Savali finally said.

"Yes. Actually. I do. I don't really understand what you are."

"I consider myself non-binary, not male or female. There are a lot of different gender identities on the spectrum, you know."

"I'm not interested in Wikipedia's definition. I want to know where you are on that spectrum."

"Fair enough. I was born a male in Samoa. I was called Fa'afafine, which is considered a third gender there. My family treated me like a girl and I fulfilled the role of daughter. When I moved to the United States, I found out that wasn't acceptable as it is in Samoa. I had to make some decisions on what gender I wanted to embrace. I went to some support groups, a couple of doctors and therapists, and experimented with dating both men and women. I realized that I was, in fact, comfortable in my body and my mind in both genders. I also realized that I could wake up on any given day and prefer to dress or behave in one or the other. In other words, I identify as both and I identify as neither. Does that make sense?"

"Sort of."

"Well, I also realized that I was happy and not the least bit conflicted over it. Even though all those doctors and therapists tried to convince me that I was a psychological mess." She took Malcolm's hand and looked deeply into his eyes. "I understand that this might be hard for you to believe, but really . . . I am very happy and at peace with who I am."

"I do believe you."

"I also understand that this is a lot for you to take in. You haven't spent a lifetime exploring your sexual identity. You can't welcome me as a lover without doing the mental work first."

"Thanks for understanding that."

"I can wait. But we cannot deny the attraction and strong feelings we have for each other."

"I'm not denying it."

"I know you're not. And I appreciate that. I'm just glad you're not trying to suppress them."

Malcolm laughed. "I don't think I could even if I wanted to."

"Yes. You could. Honestly, people do it all the time. Most people can't embrace anything out of the norm."

"Well, I still need time. And I, um, can't comfortably . . . uh, you know."

"As I said. I can wait. But, just so you know, if we have sex it doesn't make you gay. That has nothing to do with it."

"I know that!"

"I'm just a human being that you've fallen for; just as I've fallen for you as a human being, not as one gender or another. I'll go to bed in Nick's room and if you want to experiment with the sexual part of our relationship, feel free to wake me up." She got up and went to his side of the table. She squeezed his hand and kissed his cheek.

Malcolm watched her walk out of the dining room and down the hall. He sat at the table for several minutes. At first, he pondered the whole big picture of what Savali had talked about. But soon his musings turned to his own feelings and how he wanted to proceed. He got nowhere in his thoughts, however, and walked back to his own room. He paused in front of the door to where Savali slept, but he knew he was nowhere near ready to confront that whole part of this new relationship.

Sleep, however, eluded him that night. He got up several times and opened the door to his room, debating about knocking on Savali's door, even if just to talk. He certainly wouldn't talk to anyone else about this situation. He wasn't sure if it was embarrassment or even humiliation. It felt like his world was crashing down on him. He was confused about his career path, but that was easier to explore than this. He'd never been in love before but he had certainly never expected it to be anything other than a normal heterosexual relationship.

Malcolm did not slip into negative, dark thoughts very often. He was usually optimistic and at peace with himself. Up until now, he was content to just try different things and let his life's journey play out however it would. He was willing to do what it took to get where he wanted to go. And if he didn't know where that was, he had faith that it would somehow appear. But he knew his feelings for Savali were at the bottom of it all, overshadowing everything else. He had so many questions. And he knew that the only person who could help him through this was Savali. But she was the last person he wanted to talk to right now.

Malcolm hoped Savali would still be asleep when he finally gave in to his insomnia and tiptoed into the kitchen. But she was leaning against the sink with a cup of coffee in her hand. She wore a short, frilly, nightgown and smiled at him as he entered. "You're up too?" she said as she handed him the cup.

"I guess it's pervasive in this house tonight."

"It's almost dawn. We could call it this morning."

"Great. We'll spend the day walking around like zombies."

"Maybe that's a good thing." She winked at him.

"What time is it?" Malcolm looked at the clock on the microwave as he asked. "Oh, already five."

"Is it?" She stretched her arms up to the ceiling and then touched her toes, exposing her shapely bare bottom that was not flat like a man's. As much as she worked out, her arms and legs were toned and muscular, but still womanly, not overly so like a body-builder.

That was the problem. If her physique looked more masculine, maybe he wouldn't be so damn attracted to her. He turned his head away, but kept his eyes on her backside, summing up exactly how conflicted he felt. She finally stood up and went to the living room. She turned on the television and lounged on the sofa, channel-surfing on the remote. "Maybe there's a movie on we can watch?" she called to him. He stood in the doorway. "Do you get HBO or one of those stations?"

"No."

She clicked some more and stopped when Hugh Grant appeared on the screen. "How about this? Yet another fluffy, light, romantic comedy."

Malcolm hesitated and then went to the sofa and sat down next to Savali. They watched for a few minutes, neither one of them paying much attention. Finally, Savali made a move and scooted closer to him, her leg touching his. They sat like that for a few more minutes, until Malcolm put his arm around her shoulder and she turned her face toward him. They kissed and Savali lay back and pulled him to her. He didn't resist, but when she unzipped his fly, he pulled away. "Not yet, Savali. Can we just leave it at kissing for now?"

"Sure." She tried to kiss him again, but he stood up.

"I'm going to take a shower." He left hurriedly.

Savali stayed on the sofa and fantasized about what their first encounter would be like. Malcolm did the same in the shower.

29

MALCOLM DRESSED AND SNEAKED OUT THE DOOR WHILE SAVALI WAS IN THE BATHROOM GETTING READY. He could avoid her at work, and he was on that night at the cafe. He would ask to be the last one to leave, and hopefully she'd be asleep when he got home. They hadn't talked about whether she would continue to stay at his house, but he assumed she would, at least as long as Nick was not around. Maybe he'd give her a key.

It was game day, so the set up was pretty quick. Malcolm hung around in the community room, talking to various residents. Homer arrived, excited to show Malcolm how adept he had become with his smart phone. He had not only used it for web surfing, but had done some recording for a possible memoir. Homer was a fascinating guy to Malcolm. He had the best attitude and zeal for life, even after his life-changing diagnosis of Parkinson's. And it wasn't like he'd had an easy time of it before then. A carney's life was a difficult life; a roadside ritual of setting up, barking one's line, and breaking camp, over and over again. And yet, it was Homer who gushed over Malcolm.

"You are a saint, young man. This phone has opened up a whole world to me. I even found some stuff on the web about a machine that does something to your brain to stop the tremors. I don't know how much longer I can press the right buttons or whatever you call those things on the screen. It'd be great if I could find out how to get one of those machines before it's too late. Of course, it would be really expensive."

Malcolm grinned. "I'm so glad this is working for you. I'll see what I can find out about the machine. And maybe we could start a GoFundMe."

"A what?"

"It's a website to raise funds for people."

"Oh no. I wouldn't want to ask people to give me money. There are people that need money much more than I do."

"A lot of people would rather give money to a person than a big organization.

Yours is a very worthy cause. It's exactly what the fundraising should be for."

"I don't want to do that."

"Well, let me find out about the machine and then we can go from there."

Homer impetuously kissed Malcolm on the cheek. "I hope you don't mind. I'm an affectionate guy."

"I don't mind at all," Malcolm said as a flash of Savali's kisses passed through his mind. Homer went to one of the tables where they were setting up a battered, original Trivial Pursuit game. Homer had a great memory for popular culture of thirty years ago, honed during his winter down time.

Malcolm joined the poker players, but lost handily to these men who had played weekly for most of their adult lives. It was strange how the games were so divided by gender. The women had their own poker game. This whole Savali experience had Malcolm wondering about gender in general. She had certainly opened his eyes to another way of looking at it. Many other cultures had embraced more than two distinct ones. It made sense, but it was still hard to let go of norms and expectations.

"Malcolm?" He looked up, startled, to see Savali standing over him. He had been so engrossed in thought that he didn't hear her approach.

"Oh, it's you."

"Nice to see you, too."

"I—I didn't mean that the way it sounded."

"Never mind. I had an idea. Come to my office so we can talk privately."

"About us?"

"No, Malcolm," she said irritably. "It's about Nick. We still have to keep any discussion of him confidential."

"Oh, okay." He stood up and followed her to the back office. She sat in the office chair. Malcolm leaned against the wall, feeling strangely detached from the subject at hand.

"I think we should go back to San Francisco."

"What? We just got back and we had decided there was no point in looking for him."

"I know. But this just waiting around is driving me crazy, not knowing if he's dead or alive. And if he's been kidnapped, we need to do something. Here's the thing. I realized that if we call the police, he's in the clear because he is no longer part of his family's business. And honestly, do you really care if Anthony gets caught? Nick's mother is dead, so we wouldn't have to worry about her."

"I don't know. How can we be sure that Nick wouldn't also be arrested?"

"We'll vouch for him."

Malcolm laughed. "Since when are we so important that the cops would just let him go based on our accolades?"

Savali shrugged and looked out the window. After a while she murmured, "Maybe we should try to locate his son. Maybe Nick has contacted him."

"That's a good idea," Malcolm admitted. "But, do we even know his name?"

"Well, we know his last name is Balducci and he lives in San Diego. How many Balduccis can there be in San Diego?" Savali asked.

"Okay. It's a start. I'll get on one of the computers and see what I can find out."

Savali rushed toward him. "Sounds like a plan!"

Malcolm pulled back and put his hand on the doorknob. "I'm getting there. I just need a little more time."

She nodded and smiled. "I know you will." She blew him a kiss.

Malcolm went to the computer table and started Googling. There were many more Balduccis in San Diego than he thought. That city may not be known for its Italian enclave like New York or other east coast cities, but the Balducci clan apparently liked warm weather. He started copying down the names of men in their twenties when Savali came over with a look of horror on her face. "What's wrong?" he asked.

"I went to the San Francisco Chronicle website to see about the obituary for Francesca Balducci . . ." she stopped and caught her breath.

"And?" Malcolm stared at her. "What did you see?"

Savali swallowed. "There was an article about finding a body in an empty lot south of Market. A white man in his seventies with no identification. He was shot and they think it was a hit job." She swallowed again.

"Well, San Francisco's a big city . . ." Malcolm's voice trailed off.

Savali turned away abruptly and said, "I'll call the SFPD and see if they've identified him yet." She walked away. Malcolm had never seen her upset like that. Her usual assured and sarcastic manner had vanished. There was something more to her, after all. Vulnerability. It was real. It was attractive. His concerns for Nick fell further back. Here was someone here and now, in need. It fit his temperament perfectly. A desire rose in him to do more than comfort.

He went into the office and sat down. She was on the phone. "Anything?" he asked.

She talked into the phone. "You're sure of that? Okay. I'll call back to see. Thanks." She hung up and looked at Malcolm, frowning. "It fits the pattern of a typical, organized crime slaying, but they still haven't identified the body. They told me to call back later. I think it's him. Jesus!"

Malcolm wanted to take her in his arms, but didn't. His heart was pounding, but he couldn't even look at her. He just hung his head and nodded and went out. He found George, alone, in the community room, watching the game. Perfect. He needed to do something mindless to stop his thoughts going in the direction they were going and to sit next to someone who wasn't prone to talking. He sat down and feigned interest in the game by asking George what the score was. That was the end of their conversation. He just hoped none of the other guys would come around to banter with

George over the game or, worse, Violet would come to flirt. Instead, Finn entered with Kate and her husband, Martin and made a beeline for Malcolm.

Malcolm stood up and hugged Kate. "Hey, Ms. McGee. Oh, sorry. Kate!" He turned to Martin and shook his hand. "Nice to see you again." He looked at Finn. "Did you see Savali, yet?"

"Nope. She wasn't in her office. We brought some things to move into the apartment. Do I need to find her to get the key?"

"Oh, she didn't give it to you yet?"

"No. Can you let me in?"

"I can't. Maybe I can find her. Give me a minute." Malcolm went back to the office, but no Savali. He went outside to see if she was in the courtyard, and then tried each floor's hallway, but she was nowhere to be found. He saw Jose fixing someone's leaky faucet. "Have you seen Savali?"

Jose shook his head. "Not recently."

"Can you let a new resident into his apartment? He wants to move some things in."

"No can do. Not without Savali's or Annabel's okay."

"Mine's not good enough, eh?" Malcolm smiled.

"Nope." Jose winked. "Sorry. She'll be back. They should have called first." He went back to the job at hand.

Malcolm went back to the community room. "I'm sorry. I can't find her. Is it a lot of stuff? Furniture?"

"No. Just small stuff."

"We can leave it in the car and come back later," Martin added. "No problem."

"I guess you should call her and make sure she'll be here when you come. Then she can give you the key and it won't matter."

"Yeah, I should have done that." Finn turned to leave and Kate and Martin followed.

"Finn?" Malcolm called. "Could I talk to you for a minute?"

Finn looked at Kate and Martin. "I'll be right there." Malcolm and Finn walked to a corner of the room. "Any word on Nick?" Finn asked.

"That's what I wanted to tell you." He shared the information Savali had gotten from the SFPD. "She's pretty upset."

"Well, we don't know anything for sure, yet."

"No, we don't. But I think she may be out walking on the beach or something. Maybe she won't be back today."

"No problem. It's not like I have to be out of Kate and Martin's. I'll call later."

"Can we exchange numbers? We should have done that before."

"I'm not too good with my phone."

"I can show you how to work it."

"It's not that. I hate it and don't pay much attention to it. You can always call Kate's."

"I have the number but I don't think we should share all this."

"Okay. I'll try to keep the phone on me and look at it occasionally. I just don't hear it."

Malcolm took out his phone and added Finn as a contact. "Thanks. I'll text my contact info to you."

"Oh goodness, no. Just write it on a piece of paper."

"Okay. Let me find a scrap of paper."

"I've got one." Finn took an old receipt out of his pocket and handed it to Malcolm with a pen. "A writer always keeps a pen on him. You never know when the inspiration will hit." Malcolm wrote his number on the receipt. "Maybe you should call Jed."

"Why?" Malcolm asked.

"He's a good person to talk to when you need it." Finn winked and walked back to Martin and Kate. They left, and Malcolm went back to the computer to try and get more information on the chronicles of the Balducci family.

30

SAVALI NEVER SHOWED UP THAT AFTERNOON. Malcolm walked home, hoping he'd find her van parked in front, but the van was gone. He called and texted again, although he knew she probably wouldn't answer. Luckily there was another art show that night, so the cafe was busy enough to keep Malcolm distracted. It wasn't until he finished counting his cash and tipping the bussers, hostess and bartender, that his mind went to all the issues plaguing him. He wasn't surprised that the van was still gone when he got home. He went straight to bed, quickly fell asleep, and didn't wake up until morning.

It was Saturday. He would be at the boardwalk in the morning helping Charlie out and then to the children's hospital. It seemed like so long ago that he'd been to either place. He remembered one of Miss Ruthie's pet sayings: "Without confusion no clarity will

emerge. Confusion is the mother of change."
That brought a smile to his face.

It felt good to be at his old haunts. The
day went quickly with only passing thoughts of
Nick and Savali. After his shift at the Homeless
Resource table, he thought about stopping in at
Moss House to see if Finn had moved in.
Luckily, some old boardwalk denizens wanted
to talk sports and politics with him, so he didn't
have time. Deep down, he knew it was better
not to go. He gobbled down a hamburger and
rushed over to the hospital to do some baby
rocking, handholding, game playing, and to
offer his shoulder for crying for both the kids
and their parents.

He only had time for a quick shower
before he had to be at the cafe, and once again,
he was not surprised that there was no van
parked in front of his house. His worry was
tinged with a bit of anger, now. He would have
thought that she could at least answer him . . .
unless something bad had happened to her . . .
or Nick . . .

It was another good night for tips, and
he almost went with the other servers to an
after-hours bar to drink and dance. His desire to
see if Savali had shown up, however, won out.
He turned the corner onto his street, saw her

van ahead, and broke into a joyous sprint. Savali stepped out of the van when she saw him coming, and to both their surprise, he threw his arms around her and held on tightly for several minutes. When he finally let go, he took her hand and they walked through his front door to his bedroom, undressed, and got into bed without saying a word. It wasn't until they were under the covers that Malcolm finally spoke. "Show me what to do," he said without flinching.

"You're ready to do this?" Savali asked.

He took a deep breath and then answered, "Yes."

They spent most of the night exploring and experimenting. Savali told him that she left him alone because she thought it would be easier for him while he decided what he wanted to do about their relationship. He admitted that although he had been worried, angry and scared, it had been the right thing to do and they started another round.

They got out of bed at noon. Savali took a shower while Malcolm made breakfast. "Nothing like a hot shower without having to question which bathroom to use," Savali said. She sat down at the table that was laid out with a steaming cup of coffee and a hearty plate of food. "What, no breakfast in bed?" she winked as she picked up her fork and took a big bite of the omelet.

"I didn't want to clean up the crumbs," he smiled.

"You doing okay?"

"Yeah. Why?"

"You made a big leap last night into unfamiliar territory. Just wanted to make sure." They smiled at each other in between bites, but didn't say much. "I'll do the dishes," she said as she took their plates into the kitchen. "Anything new at the old people's home?" she called from the kitchen.

"Finn was by yesterday with Kate and her husband. He's ready to move in and needs the key. He gave me his and Kate's number. I told him I'd call him."

"I guess I should stop by work anyway since I haven't been there for a couple of days. Why don't you call him and tell him I'll meet him there in an hour."

"Okay. I'll go with you," Malcolm said as he took out his phone.

"Why? You don't need to."

"They might need someone to move the heavy stuff. They're all over the age of sixty."

Savali looked at him and shook her head. "Hey, doofus, I'm the bodybuilder here."

"Well, yeah, but I'm sure an extra pair of hands would be appreciated. What is it? You don't want me to come?" Malcolm looked at her, bewildered.

"Of course I do. I just thought you might want some time alone to organize your thoughts."

"I'd rather be with you." He smiled. He liked this being in love stuff. It was a new and strange feeling and it certainly had not been the kind of love interest that he had ever imagined. But now that the first hurdle had been jumped, he was more at ease with his decision.

When they arrived at Moss House, Finn saw something was up right off the bat. He gave Malcolm a lascivious wink. Savali handed over Finn's key and glided back to her office with the pride of a conqueror. "Well, I'm glad you waited until we got back from San Francisco," Finn smirked. "That futon in her van was hard as a rock!" Malcolm felt heat rise over his face, but bravely looked back at him. Finn's face softened with compassion. "Relax. Enjoy."

"Hi, Malcolm! Great to see you again!" Martin and Kate appeared carrying boxes, and in short order they had Finn's new apartment crowded with Finn's life that may or may not ever get unpacked.

"Now for the big stuff," Finn puffed. But it turned out to be only a desk, bed and a couple of comfortable chairs that Malcolm and Martin moved in short order. "I'd offer you a shot of whiskey, but Kate's got her eagle eye on me."

"Hey, not on the job," grinned Malcolm.

"Some other time. After hours. The three of us."

"And I'll bring something that won't kill me."

"Oh, you can't leave Savali out of this."

Malcolm rushed downstairs to Savali's office. "Done already?" she asked, looking up from a pile of neglected paperwork.

"Done. Not much to it. And I was motivated."

"Oh, you were, were you?"

"Yeah. No work tonight."

"That's what you think."

31

SAVALI WAS ALREADY GONE BY THE TIME MALCOLM WOKE UP. This time, however, she left a note saying that she was going to Muscle Beach before work and that she would see him later. He took his time getting ready but still got to Moss House before Savali. He was beginning to understand that the hours required for the job were flexible. And now that things were set up, he was only needed for the occasional computer and phone tutoring. Yet, the lull of the routine and the sexual release did not quite dispel his need to plan out his life.

Violet approached and took his arm. "Malcolm, honey, you need to come upstairs with me."

"Violet, you know that's not going to happen," Malcolm smiled wanly.

"No, no. I don't mean it like that. It's Homer. He's had a bad turn this weekend."

"What do you mean?"

"Just come up with me. We've all been taking turns getting him his meals, but he needs to see a doctor or something. He needs you to make him go. George tried to convince him, but he just gets his knickers in a knot and won't budge."

Malcolm ran up the stairs two at a time, leaving Violet in the dust. He got to Homer's apartment and tried the door. It was open, and George was standing at the sink washing dishes. "What's going on, Homer?" Malcolm asked breathlessly. But as soon as he saw Homer sitting at the table, he could see for himself. His hands were shaking uncontrollably and his head was wobbling back and forth.

"It's a bitch!" Homer slurred the words and spoke much slower than usual.

"You need to see the doctor. What time is it?" Malcolm said to no one as he looked at his phone screen. "The office should be open now. What's your doctor's name?"

"He won't tell us," George called from the kitchen. "We've been trying to get it out of him all weekend. He's being a stubborn prick!"

"Homer, maybe the doc can give you a different medicine or up the dose of what you're taking. Why won't you go?"

"No!"

Malcolm looked around the room for Homer's phone. He had helped put in the contacts. He remembered seeing a couple of doctors' names. He went into the bedroom, but it wasn't in there either. He probably had it in his pocket. Malcolm returned to the living room. "I can stay with him, George, if you want to go. And Violet's on her way up."

"Yeah. Good luck with that. She has to proposition every man on her way!" Malcolm wondered if Violet had ever propositioned Savali and laughed out loud. "What's funny? It's a pain in the ass," George retorted.

"Yeah. I know it is." George left and Malcolm turned back to Homer. "What are you going to do, then?"

"Help me downstairs." His answer took a whole minute to come out.

Malcolm helped him up and positioned him on his walker. It took almost ten minutes just to get to the elevator. "Where's your phone, Homer?"

"No."

"I won't call your doctor. I promise. I have another idea."

Homer tried to put his hand in his pocket, but he was trembling so much that he kept missing it. Malcolm finally reached in and took out the phone. He looked for Pandora and found a blues station. He turned it on and watched Homer's face. "Wha–."

"Just listen. I saw this on YouTube." They stood in the hall, listening quietly to the music for a minute or two. Homer started humming along and then Malcolm said, "Try walking down the hall."

Homer stared at him, puzzled, but then took a step, pushing his walker. His gait got faster and his humming got louder. He went up and down the hall several times and on each trip his stride got smoother. Soon he was able to leave the walker behind. When the song was over, he beamed at Malcolm.

Malcolm grinned back and took his arm. "Let's go downstairs. I have to set up the tables for Arts and Crafts. Do you have any headphones?"

"No."

"Then would you rather go back to your apartment and keep the music on? I'll buy you some at lunchtime."

"Yes."

Malcolm helped him back to his apartment and got him situated in his chair. "You can practice your dancing this morning. I'll be back after I set up the community room."

"Okay."

Malcolm left and found Violet talking to a UPS delivery driver, her arm linked in his and her eyelids fluttering. Malcolm smiled and shook his head. He started moving furniture and soon the tables were covered with yarn skeins, beads, watercolor palettes, and mosaic tiles, while every chair was filled with eager artists and craftspeople. Since Malcolm's interests didn't run to creating home decor, he took the opportunity to check on Homer.

He opened the door to his apartment and found Homer singing, dancing, and grinning. He looked fluid in his movements and his voice was clear and strong. Malcolm took his hands and they danced around together, grinning, for a few moments. When the song ended, Homer sat down in his chair and said, "Music is very powerful."

"In many ways," Malcolm answered. Homer nodded and closed his eyes as the next song came on. His hands and head were still, and the smile had not left his face. Malcolm watched him for a minute, and when Homer's breathing turned into snoring, he tiptoed out.

Savali was standing at the reception desk talking to George when Malcolm got to the bottom of the stairs. "Hi Malcolm, how are you today?" She spoke as if she hadn't seen him in days. "George just filled me in on Homer's condition."

"I just left him and he's doing very well."

"Did you talk him into going to the doctor?" George asked.

"Nope. Turned on Pandora."

"What are you talking about?"

"You know how playing the piano helps his tremors? Well, I thought it was only about the focusing, but it's the music too. I saw something on YouTube and it showed this physical therapist using music to help a Parkinson's patient walk more rapidly and without shuffling. I tried it with Homer and you wouldn't believe it! He was singing and dancing without shaking at all!"

George shook his head and said, "Ain't that something!"

Savali's smile covered her face from ear to ear. "Ain't *you* something!"

"Well, it's not like a cure but it does help him temporarily."

"How do you know it's not a cure?" she asked.

"I, uh, guess I don't. Well, it gives him some relief and that's good. Did he talk to you about going to the gym with you, George, to try boxing? That's supposed to work too."

"Yeah. He talked about it."

"I'm going to get him some ear buds, so he can listen to music outside of his apartment."

"Malcolm! We need you!" a voice came out of the community room.

"You're in demand," Savali winked. "I guess you're indispensable, after all."

"Yeah, right."

Malcolm got the ear buds at lunchtime and brought back sandwiches for him and Savali. The afternoon was spent cleaning up the community room and then giving tutorials on the computers. They were pretty outdated, but you could get on the Internet and most of the residents just wanted to learn how to make a Facebook page, how to Google, and how to watch YouTube videos. He had already set up email accounts for most of them, but they were stubborn about deleting old mail. Some of them had to be convinced that they didn't need to hang on to five hundred emails that they had already read.

Malcolm stopped by the front desk when he left at four. Savali was on the phone and when he raised his eyebrows and cocked his head toward the door, his way of asking if she wanted to walk home with him, she waved him off.

It wasn't until much later when he was on his way home from the cafe, looking forward to another enjoyable night frolicking in bed, that it dawned on him that he had not given Savali a key to his house. Hopefully, she was waiting in her van parked in front. He peeked in the driver's side and passenger's side windows, and then knocked on the back door when he didn't see her. No answer. Maybe she was sleeping. He started to worry about her being cold, but then remembered that she had spent many a night in her van. He opened his front door and found her reading on the couch. "Hey," he smiled at her.

"Hey."

"How'd you get in?"

"I have my ways."

"Yes. You are beguiling."

"You trying to impress me with your big words?"

"Nope." He sat down and took her hand in his. "You're the impressive one. You amaze me with how grounded and self-assured you are."

"Why do you say that?"

"Most people would be struggling with their sexual identity more. You seem to have accepted that you are . . . hmm . . . want to make sure I use the correct term . . . non-binary gender? Is that the right one?"

"I told you. It doesn't matter what you call me. Transgender, third gender, non-binary gender, no gender . . . but you're right. I am totally at peace with who I am."

"How? It's still hard for me to accept that I'm sleeping with a DMAB. Did I get the right acronym? Designated male at birth?"

"Yes. For one thing, I've been dealing with it all my life and remember, in Samoa, it's no big deal. That's my background and that gave me a big head start when I moved here."

"That's true." Malcolm sighed. "So it's not put on? You really are that content?"

"I guess I am. Are you?"

"Happy with who I am? Well, I'm not unhappy. I guess I'm confused and maybe a little scared."

"Scared of what?"

"The future."

"What's to be scared of? Us? Falling in love with a transgender?"

"That. And also what I'm going to do, you know, career-wise."

Savali laughed. "You'll be fine. 'Que Sera, Sera,' 'Don't Worry Be Happy.' Our lives are defined by song titles!"

"It's like Homer said, 'Music is powerful.' Maybe I should pay more attention to it."

"So now you're going to be a musician?"

Malcolm laughed. "That would be a stretch, since I don't even know how to play an instrument."

"Never too late to learn. How to play an instrument . . . how to have sex with a boy when you're not homosexual." She raised her eyebrows at him and tilted her head.

He smiled. "Okay. I get it. Enough conversation." He stood and took her hand and pulled her up. They undressed and got into bed. Savali started to kiss him, but Malcolm pulled away. "Could I ask one favor of you, though?"

"What's that?" she cooed at him.

"I know at work you dress pretty much unisex. And I see that you seem to go with whatever your mood is other times."

"It's how I feel that day, whether I feel male or female."

"When we go out together, could you dress like a female? At least for now."

Savali was quiet for a minute. "You know that means you're not accepting who I am."

"Yes. I know that. But I think it would help nudge me along if you would do that for me. Just for a while." He took a deep breath. "This is hard for me. You said before that you were helped because of your background in Samoa. Well, I'm a black man from Texas who was adopted by a woman who made him go to church every Sunday, and was taught that homosexuality is a sin."

Savali's shoulders dropped with her defenses. "Oh, Malcolm, you know that's bullshit," she shot back angrily. "First of all, the devil hasn't risen between us in bed. Secondly, you're a sensitive adult. Live by your heart. Look where all that teaching got you. Right here. With me!"

"Hey, hold on. I'm not excusing it. I'm just saying it makes it harder."

Savali took a breath. "Anyway, you're not homosexual. You fell in love with a transgender as a female. If you had never seen me dressed as a woman, would you have given me a second thought?"

Malcolm laughed. "You're not easy to ignore!"

"You know what I mean."

"Yes. I fell in love with the female you."

"Yet you knew all along that was only a part of me."

"Savali, I've had relationships before, but you are the first person I've allowed myself to fall in love with. This was not what I expected."

"Me neither." Malcolm gave her a puzzled look. "I've had sex with both men and women, but I've never felt like this before, either. It's new for me, too. So I'm going to ride my high horse sidesaddle for a while. I don't like being told what to do, but I'll give you this 'woman by your side' a trial run. I love you and I want to work on this relationship together. But realize I'll dress as I damn well please when I'm alone. And people will notice, just as they always have, that I am my own person. Get used to it."

32

AFTER SEVERAL WEEKS OF LEARNING HOW TO LOVE EACH OTHER AND HOW TO LIVE WITH EACH OTHER, SAVALI OFFICIALLY MOVED IN. They didn't tell anyone at Moss House, but like most new lovers, it was obvious to everyone. Finn didn't help matters by teasing them mercilessly and not always out of earshot of the others. Most of them were oblivious to the fact that Savali was male, anyway. Those few that thought she was male just assumed they'd been wrong about Malcolm and he was gay. Not that anyone cared enough to make it an issue.

Now that things with Savali had settled into a routine of sorts, Malcolm went back to being preoccupied with his career prospects. Finn had taken over the writing workshop and turned it into a real class where one could learn the craft, not just share their own musings. Malcolm had become an avid attendee, and took his assignments very seriously. Finn had assigned a 700-word biography one week, and Malcolm ended up with three times that and could have written more. He was surprised at how easily the words came, but more than that, he was surprised at how good it felt.

One afternoon he was working with Finn on downloading music from iTunes in the community room and said, "I'm really enjoying the writing workshop."

"I know you are, but I don't think it's because you want to write a book."

"What do you mean? How can you know that?"

Finn winked at him. "You didn't know I was omniscient?"

"But I like writing."

"I didn't say you didn't. But you're using the writing prompts to help figure yourself out. That's a good thing and what you should be doing right now. You have plenty of time to write a book. I didn't start until I retired."

Malcolm sighed. "Maybe you're right."

"You've had quite an awakening with Savali."

Malcolm looked at Finn warily. He really didn't want to have his conversation. "Um, yes, but . . ."

"Savali is a fascinating creature."

Malcolm laughed. "Creature?"

"Okay, maybe it wasn't a good choice of word. But you and I both know she's pretty special. She has a lot to offer people who are not so understanding of their own sexuality and gender determination."

"Yeah." Malcolm still didn't know where Finn was headed.

"You're a videographer, right?"

"I guess so."

"Why not make a documentary about Savali. I can help you write it and my son-in-law, Martin, has some Hollywood connections and I understand you do too."

Malcolm laughed. "Well, sort of. I was asked to shoot a porno film."

Finn burst out laughing. "You?! Well, didn't you intern with some bigwigs too?"

"I know a couple of people, I guess."

"So think about it. Talk to Savali."

"I guess I could talk to her." Malcolm went back to downloading, but his mind was a million miles away. Actually, he loved the idea, but he doubted Savali would. It would be a huge thing to ask someone: to put themselves on display like that. He would need to approach it with her gently and show her the political importance of getting this out to the public to further the LGBT agenda. She should respond to that, since she had been eager to find out about the Oregon non-binary gender law.

He stopped by the office when he was ready to leave. "Want to go out to dinner tonight? I don't have to work."

"Okay, but what's the occasion?"

"Let's see. How about just celebrating us?"

"That's good enough for me. But first I'll need to go home and change into my girly clothes," she added pointedly.

Malcolm chose to ignore rather than react to her sarcasm. She wasn't going to let him forget that his wardrobe requirement was supposed to be temporary. "Can you leave now or should I meet you at home?"

"I'll see you in about half an hour. I have to finish up something."

Malcolm looked around him and saw that no one was in the vicinity, so he blew her a kiss. He left and jogged home, not just because he was excited at Finn's suggestion, but also because he wanted to get home to do some Googling.

He was at his computer when Savali came in. She peeked into his room and saw him engrossed so she jumped into the shower. She decided to go overboard on her outfit to express her resentment over the arrangement, even though she enjoyed being a woman in his company.

"I'm ready." She appeared at the door, dressed to kill, in high heels and a black cocktail dress. For someone who worked out as much as she did, and being physically male, she kept her muscle definition to a minimum by carefully crafting her exercise routine.

"Wow! Gorgeous! I'll be ready in a few." He jumped up and got ready and they were out the door in twenty minutes. He wore a suit, just in keeping with the charade. "The way we're dressed, we'll need to go big time. Any requests?"

"Yes. Let's go to Santa Monica. I'll even drive," Savali said.

"I can drive."

"Why? Got to be the macho man?"

"C'mon, Savali. Let's not keep joking around about it. I offered because I know you don't like to drive in the city."

"Okay. But I'll drive." They got in the van, but it wouldn't start. "Shit! Now what?"

"We'll deal with it tomorrow. Let's just walk over to Abbot Kinney and find a nice place to eat."

"I'll freeze walking all the way there in this dress. Let's just go to Chaya."

"Yeah, sushi sounds good."

"So, what do you want to talk about?" Savali asked as they walked.

"Why do you think I want to talk about something specific?"

"Oh, c'mon Malcolm. We may not have know each other that long, but I know you well."

He put his arm around her. "You do. But let's wait until we're at the restaurant."

It wasn't a long walk and they were soon sitting at a table with a bottle of Sake in front of them. "So, what's up?" Savali took a sip and sat back in her chair.

"I'd like to make a documentary."

"Great. About what?"

He swallowed and took a breath. "You."

"Me? What are you talking about?"

"Well, about transgender or third genders or whatever . . . I haven't thought it through that much. Finn gave me the idea this afternoon. But you would be such a great role model for people struggling with their gender and sexual identity. And we could make a real statement on the whole issue." Savali just stared at him, frowning. "You don't have to say anything right now. Just think about it."

The rest of dinner was spent with Malcolm excitedly sharing all he had researched and how he wanted to approach the film. Savali just listened and nodded her head at the appropriate moments, so he wouldn't notice that she hadn't said anything. He didn't stop talking until they got home and into bed and began their lovemaking.

33

MALCOLM WAS ON THE PHONE WHEN SAVALI GOT UP. After he hung up, he kissed her and said, "That was an old army buddy of mine in New York. He works for PBS, and I wanted to give him a heads up, in case he has any ideas or any advantageous connections. He suggested I start a GoFundMe or Kickstarter campaign."

"I haven't agreed yet."

"I know. But it just feels good to be excited about something, to feel like I have a direction."

"So you'd be okay if I said no?"

Malcolm's jaw dropped. He tried to hide his disappointment. "Of course."

"I'm not saying no," she added quickly. "I just don't want you to get so into this and then it might not happen."

Malcolm sat down and smiled. "It's more about making a documentary. If not about you, I'll find something or someone else. Don't worry." He took her hand. "I'll focus my research on figuring out how I'm going to pay for it."

"Good idea. Now, I'm late for my workout."

"I thought you just went when you felt like it."

"I have buddies there. I meet them and we work out together." She went toward the bathroom and called over her shoulder, "I won't be long."

Malcolm sat motionless. He knew she would take her time to decide, but he hadn't really thought she might actually say no. His mood turned sour. This was not how he thought this day would start.

He avoided Savali at work, which wasn't hard to do, since she was apparently avoiding him as well. And Finn was keeping him busy putting his apartment in order. Malcolm hadn't realized that Kate had been in Los Angeles only for a short visit before returning to the Peace Corps. Although he was spry and healthy, Finn wasn't particularly domestic or handy. He didn't know how to do the simplest tasks and had no interest in learning how. But he was encouraging and resourceful, and most of all, happy to listen to Malcolm's ideas. And

Malcolm was happy to share them with someone who could be excited with him.

Savali was sleeping when Malcolm got home from the cafe, and either didn't wake up when he got into bed, or pretended she was still asleep. And she would leave especially early in the morning. A few days went by without seeing each other, until finally it was Saturday.

"Good morning," Malcolm said when Savali returned home from Muscle Beach. He didn't have to be at the Homeless Resource Table that morning because Charlie was training some of the homeless people staying at the shelter to man the table. Malcolm would just be the back up when needed.

She smiled and kissed him on the cheek. "Been a while."

"Yes. Maybe it's time to talk."

"Before we go into anything too heavy, have you checked on Nick's whereabouts at all?" she asked.

"How would I do that?"

"Like you had been doing. You know, online, seeing what you can find out."

"Well, you could do that too."

"I did."

"Then why are you asking me?" Malcolm was more irritated than curious, but also a little guilty that he hadn't given Nick much thought lately. "Did you find out anything?"

Savali shook her head. "Nope. He's disappeared. I even called the San Francisco police as well as checked the hospitals and the obituaries. Nothing."

"Well, maybe that's good news."

"Malcolm, the eternal optimist."

He didn't think it was a good time to bring up the documentary. "I have to work tonight, but how about going out to dinner tomorrow?"

"Okay. Aren't you late for your shift on the boardwalk?"

"I don't need to go today. I'm going to the children's hospital this afternoon."

"What time do you have to leave?"

"In about an hour."

"Do you want to have some make-up sex?" she asked.

He smiled. "I didn't know we were fighting."

"Well, no I guess we weren't. But that doesn't have to stop us from having make-up sex."

"No, it doesn't," he said as he took her hand.

Malcolm's afternoon in the children's cancer ward served to take his mind off everything else. How well these kids accepted their disease was inspiring. The ones who weren't too sick, who could laugh and play, drew him into their carefree world. And that was just what he needed, both to bring him up from his bewildered brooding about his relationship with Savali, and to bring him down from his euphoric daydreaming about his newfound career of filmmaking.

Savali wasn't home when he returned to shower and dress for work, and she was asleep when he got home at midnight. Another day and night went by without seeing much of each other.

Malcolm spent most of Sunday emailing or phoning anyone he could think of that might help him on his new path. He rekindled some old relationships in the entertainment business and found a great deal of interest in his subject matter. He knew he was getting a bit ahead of himself since Savali had not agreed yet, but he had faith that she would come around. And anyway, it's not like he had signed any contracts yet. He could always find something or someone else to do a documentary on. Maybe he could do Nick's story, or Homer's; both of those were also interesting. Of course, he couldn't do Nick's without finding him . . .

Savali had been gone most of the day, working out at the gym as well as Muscle Beach. It was close to five when she returned. "What time are we going to dinner?" she asked.

"I don't know. When do you want to go?" he replied.

"I don't care. Seven?"

"That's fine." He glanced at her quickly and smiled and then purposely returned his gaze to his computer screen. He wanted to wait until dinner when she would have relaxed a bit from the wine and good food.

She stared at him a minute, standing at the door to the bedroom, and then went into the bathroom to shower. Malcolm closed the lid to his laptop at six and took his own shower. He didn't put on a suit, but he had on some khakis and a button-down shirt, assuming Savali would be dressed to the nines. When he went into the living room after six thirty, he was surprised to see Savali dressed in jeans and a long sleeved T-shirt. Her hair was in a bun, finalizing the male hipster look. "Oh," he said tentatively.

"Oh? What's that mean?"

"Um, nothing. Uh, are you ready?"

She stood up and put on a black blazer. "Yes. Where are we going?" Malcolm didn't answer and didn't move. "Hello? Earth to Malcolm."

He stared at her. He wanted to tell her to change her clothes, but he knew she was making a statement, and that he really didn't have any right to tell her how to dress. But they did have an agreement. "I thought, um, that I asked you . . ."

"She looked down at her clothes. "These can go either way, can't they?"

"I guess."

"This is what I felt like wearing. Just don't hold my hand if you're uptight. We can just be a couple of guys having dinner together."

Malcolm shrugged. "Okay." This wasn't boding well for the outcome of their future conversation.

They went to a casual Thai restaurant. This wasn't the wining and dining that Malcolm had hoped to do. Their conversation was stilted and stayed within the parameters of small talk. When their dishes were removed and the check was placed between them on the table, Savali grabbed it. "I'll pay. You did last time."

Malcolm sighed. He knew exactly what she was doing. He liked paying for their dinners out. It gave him the semblance of a normal male-female relationship. "Fine. Do you want to go get a drink somewhere to talk?" He knew it might be a bad idea, since she was making it so obvious that she was probably not going to go along with the documentary. But he wanted to know once and for all and he still thought it was better to have the conversation out instead of back home.

"Sure. Let's go to the brewery we went to on our first date."

Now what was she doing. Breaking up with him? Going to the same place as their first date for their last one? "If you want." They walked silently to the Ale House and Malcolm got them two beers at the bar, while Savali found a table. He set the beers down, sat down, and took a large swig. "Well? What do you want to do?"

"About what?" she answered.

"The documentary. Or did you want to talk about something else."

"Well, talking about the documentary means talking about a lot of things, doesn't it?"

"I guess it does. But can we just cut to the chase and give me an answer, yes or no. Then we can elaborate on the rest."

She sighed and shook her head. "It isn't cut and dry, Malcolm. You're asking me to expose my whole life in front of a large audience."

"Yes, but for a great cause. One that I know you believe in, strongly."

"Of course I do. But . . ."

"Don't you want to make a difference for the LGBT community? You are so self-assured and at peace with yourself as a Trans or whatever you want me to call it. I think it would help a lot of people to see your story."

"Malcolm, you don't have to preach to me. It's not about that. It's about my whole life changing. That's what would happen if I became the spokesperson or the role model or whatever."

Malcolm couldn't answer that one. He knew she was right. This could definitely change her life. And he hadn't even thought about the fact that ultimately it would also change his. He would be the heterosexual man with a transgender male. Maybe he also needed to think this through a bit. He sat back in his chair and grinned at her. "You have a point."

She grinned back. "Thanks."

He took her hand, and for the first time he didn't care what anybody thought.

34

MALCOLM KEPT HIS PLANS FOR THE DOCUMENTARY TO HIMSELF FOR THE NEXT SEVERAL DAYS. He researched and promoted it with his old entertainment business friends. He talked about it with Finn, but never brought it up with Savali. She was caught up in her own sleuthing on the Internet when they were home together and she didn't share what she was researching with Malcolm either. This made for a calm and pleasant household.

Homer had given up on the idea of going to the gym. Music and dancing in his own apartment had given him some control over his balance and trembling. Violet and George had taken him under their wing, and George used his own boxing knowledge to coach Homer through some moves in the community room.

Finn found Violet's coquetry amusing so between Homer and Finn, she wasn't honing in on Malcolm anymore, or anyone else, for that matter. That made Finn very popular with the male residents, maybe even more than the impression of a famous author in their midst. Finn relished the attention from all of them and made the most of it. He had ulterior motives, though. The women cooked meals for him and the men invited him out for drinks. And Malcolm, who hung on Finn's every word, took the place of the grandson he never had.

Savali stayed in her office most of the day, which wasn't unusual, but now was a little disconcerting for Malcolm. She seemed distant both at work and at home, although not in their lovemaking. Finally one afternoon he knocked on the office door and entered. "Hey. We haven't really talked much lately. I just wondered what you've been up to. You seem to be doing a lot of web surfing. Looking for Nick?"

"Some."

"Maybe we should make more of an effort to really be with each other when we're at home."

"That would be difficult for you. You work so much that you don't have any other time to be on your computer," Savali said.

"Actually, I could sneak in some time in the afternoons when I'm here."

"Malcolm, don't worry about it."

He shrugged and started to leave. Then he turned around. "I'm off tonight. Dinner out?"

"Sure. I'll be home about six," she answered as she turned back toward her computer screen and started typing.

Malcolm wasn't sure how to take her attitude, but he was determined to talk to her that night about everything. Maybe she had just been waiting for him to start the conversation. He wanted to get moving on the documentary, and if she wasn't going to agree to do it, he had to find someone else. She probably knew others in the transgender community, and he was sure there were some who were more politically motivated than Savali. There would surely be people who would relish having their life made into a movie. But what would that sharp focus on another do to their relationship? And where was this relationship going? He decided to walk on the beach.

He was oblivious to the scores of tourists surrounding him on the boardwalk. He veered onto the sand and walked south toward the Venice Pier. He realized he hadn't given much thought to the future of their relationship. He seemed to have moved past the social misgivings of making love to a person with male body parts. He was attracted to Savali's feminine side and that seemed to be enough for him. But was this how he wanted the rest of his life to go? Never again making love to a woman? Never having biological children? He couldn't say that he wanted that to happen. He was in love with her, but was he ready to give all that up?

He checked the time on his phone and jogged back to Moss House. By the time he got back, Savali had already left and he was not going to get home by six. "Sorry I'm late," he called out as he entered the living room. "I'll be ready in a minute." He hadn't really noticed Savali sitting on the sofa and just ran into the bedroom to change clothes. When he returned to the living room, he saw that she had on the same clothes that she had on that first night in the cafe when she was on the date with Byron. His face lit up, and he literally had to catch his breath. "Wow! You look gorgeous!" he said when he finally got a hold of himself.

"Thanks. Where to?"

"I don't know. Any preference?"

"Italian. In honor of Nick."

"Okay. Where?"

"Cassariano?"

"A little steep. Who's buying?" Malcolm then caught himself. "Just kidding."

"We'll go Dutch." She took his arm and once again he felt the rush of warmth and sensuality throughout his body that had started this whole thing some months ago.

They ordered a bottle of wine and finished it before the main course was served so they ordered another. By the time the waiter arrived with the dessert menus, they were uninhibited enough to discuss all of it, and there was still half a bottle of wine left if they need to fortify themselves any further.

"Well, how shall we begin?" Savali asked.

"I'll go," Malcolm answered. "Let's start with the documentary. But then I want to talk about us. We need to have that discussion either way. It's just that the direction will be different depending on whether or not you say yes or no to doing the film."

"Okay. Yes."

Malcolm jumped out of his chair and kissed Savali on the lips, surprising both of them. He had never done anything like that in public. Of course, no one in the restaurant knew Savali was physically male, or at least that's what Malcolm thought, so it felt safe. He sat back down and poured more wine into both their glasses, and then lifted his. "To us and a great collaboration."

Savali looked at him skeptically, but toasted him anyway. "Before we go into the logistics of how we are going to make this documentary, I want to lay out a few ground rules."

Now it was Malcolm's turn to look skeptically at her. "Ground rules?"

"Maybe that's not the right way to say it. Not in terms of the documentary, but in terms of our relationship."

He sat back in his chair. "What do you mean?"

"I need to recognize and validate my masculine side. I agreed to dressing as a female when we go out, but I think it's been long enough. It's only fair that I get to be me . . . the authentic me . . . not the one that pleases others. Especially since you say I am a role model and this film is all about my self-assurance. Well, who I am is not necessarily always a woman."

"I know. I understand. I really do. And I'm okay with it. But, I just want you to know that I'm still struggling with how I want to proceed in the relationship."

"Fair enough. We'll see where it goes."

Malcolm felt that knot in his stomach, but he took another sip of wine and said, "Now can I tell you my ideas for the documentary?"

"Shoot." And they sat at the table until the restaurant closed, and this time Savali was a willing and even eager participant in the discussion. They returned home and fell asleep after a lazy attempt at sex, thanks to the two bottles of wine.

35

MALCOLM THREW HIMSELF INTO CREATING THE DOCUMENTARY. Having spent several sleepless nights planning it out in his head, he scrawled out the storyboard in less than an hour. Savali looked it over. "It's okay as an outline, Malcolm, but you need to do more research and talk to some people . . . a lot of people."

"What do you mean?"

"I mean you've written about me, but I am just one little blip on the continuum. You need to interview some others."

"Okay. I get it. So?"

"So what?"

"You gonna find me some more non-binary gender people to interview?" He grinned.

"No."

"Huh? Why not?"

"This is your documentary. You're the producer. I'm just the star." Savali struck a pose and batted her eyelashes at him.

"C'mon Savali. I'm sure you could help me out here."

"Nope. I'm going to Muscle Beach for my workout. See you later." She left, ignoring Malcolm's protests.

He looked up LGBT organizations online and found a bunch of Meetups in Los Angeles. There was one group getting together that night in North Hollywood. They were called The Gender Fluid Dance Collective and they met twice a month at various clubs in the LA area. He would have to ask Savali to borrow her van to get there, but he secretly hoped she would go with him. He knew they would be more comfortable talking to him about their experiences if she was there too.

He went to work and tried to talk to Savali, but she holed up in her office and every time Malcolm went to knock on her door, she was on the phone and waved him away. He wasn't sure if this was by design, or she was actually that busy. When the afternoon was over, he opened her door and peeked his head in. "Want to walk home together?" he asked.

"Sorry. I'm swamped with work. I'll see you in a couple of hours."

"A couple of hours? Like seven o'clock?"

She grinned at him. "You'll manage without me."

"I know, but I wanted to see if —"

"I'm really busy, Malcolm," she interrupted.

Malcolm left, feeling dejected. He picked up some dinner at Whole Foods on his way and waited for Savali to get home to eat. He showered and dressed and watched the clock. The Meetup was scheduled to start at eight, and it would take at least forty-five minutes to get there. It was now seven and he realized he'd better eat and look for the keys to the van. Savali was probably not going to be going with him. Apparently, she knew that when she left this morning, because he found the keys in a very conspicuous place. She knew him well. When he made up his mind to do something, he did it right away. He wolfed down his dinner, left a note on the table telling her where he went and that her dinner was in the fridge, and left to battle the traffic on the 405.

He got to the club after eight. The neighborhood was a bit sketchy and the club a real working class dive bar, a far cry from the "hip" Venice Beach tourist traps. The music had already begun, which surprised him. Then he remembered that it was a Monday night, so things got under way earlier. The group on the dance floor was motley and small. There were only about seven people and Malcolm struggled to figure out their place on the gender spectrum. There were a few people sitting at the bar and tables, but he assumed they were not part of the collective. He sat at the bar and waited for the song that was playing to stop so he could approach the group and explain what he wanted. But that was not to be, for the music mixed into one song after another. It was a good half hour or so before the band and the dancers took a break. They went en masse to a table covered with glasses and Malcolm got up and sauntered over, trying to look cool.

"Hey, may I join you?" he asked. They nodded and one of them patted a chair, motioning him to sit. "I looked you up on the Meetup site. I'm making a documentary and I'd like to ask you some questions."

They glanced at each other and then back at him, warily. Finally one of them spoke. "A documentary about what?"

"LGBT . . . uh . . ." He stumbled trying to find the best words. "Non-binary gender choices? You know, like the transgender experience." Their expressions turned stony, and he tried to remedy his bad first impression. "It's about my friend who is Fa'afafine, a third gender from Samoa, but I wanted some other perspectives." This seemed to work. They all relaxed and a couple of them even smiled.

"What do you want to know?"

"I'm not sure." He decided to be honest. "Actually, it was my friend's idea that I get other people's viewpoints and experiences."

"Who wants to be interviewed?" one of them asked the others. A couple of people shook their heads, a couple of them smirked and shrugged, but a couple did agree with a wave of their hands. "I'll do it too," said the one who had asked the question.

"Great!" Malcolm was thrilled to get three people. But then the music started again and all of them except the vocal one got up to dance.

"I'll go first," he said. At least Malcolm thought it was a "he" but he wasn't going to jump to any conclusions. "Do you have specific questions or do you want me to just talk?"

"It's kind of loud. Can we get away from the music? I'd like to videotape if that's okay with you. I have my camera in my van. We could do it in there. I'm Malcolm, by the way."

"Avery." They shook hands. "This is a little suspect, though."

"Suspect? What do you mean?" Malcolm asked.

Avery smiled. "You want me to go to your van with you? You're not looking for sex? Maybe you're transphobic and want to kill me."

"Oh no! God no!" Malcolm sputtered. "I'm sorry. I can see that you might think that. Is there anything I can do to reassure you?"

"I don't know. Do you have any credentials?"

"I can show you my driver's license." He took out his wallet. "Oh wait . . . here." He handed Avery his Local 600 International Cinematographers Guild card.

"That helps." Avery handed Malcolm back the card and followed Malcolm out and down the street to where the van was parked. Malcolm opened the back door and Avery peered inside. "Do you live in this?"

"No. It's my friend, Savali's. She's the one I'm doing the documentary about."

"Where is she?"

"Probably at my house. She lives there now."

Avery raised his eyebrows. "Oh?"

Malcolm quickly changed the subject. "You can sit here on the futon. It'll take me a minute to get the camera up and running. Avery got in and sat on the futon while Malcolm took out the camera and knelt in front of him. After a few false starts when the camera angle and the lighting had to be adjusted, Avery requested that Malcolm ask a couple of questions at first. "How do you describe yourself?"

"Transgender. I was born female but identify as male."

"Have you had surgery?"

"No. I don't feel the need. And if I had," Avery added pointedly, "I would have said 'transsexual'."

"Do you want to be referred to as 'he' or 'she'?"

Avery smiled. "What did you think when you met me?"

"You were male."

"Well, then."

"So the answer is that you'd like to be referred to as 'he'?"

"Actually, I prefer 'they'."

"They?" Malcolm looked bewildered.

"Yeah."

"But that would be very confusing."

"So what?"

"Okay. When did you know?"

"When did I know what? That I wanted to be referred to as 'they'?"

"No. Sorry. I meant that you were transgender."

Avery looked away for a minute and then shrugged. "I always knew. I don't know. As a young child."

"Do you sleep primarily with men or women?"

"I sleep with women." Avery started to relax and was able to continue the interview without Malcolm's questions. He/she/they just opened up, explaining how and when they came out to their family and friends, and what it was like at work for them. They also shared their slow awakening to the fact that they was not just attracted to other women, but also that they identified male. The conversation lasted half an hour and Malcolm was fascinated with how different the viewpoint and gender identification were from Savali. He finally understood what Savali meant when she said she was 'gender-fluid'." Avery gave Malcolm their number as they climbed out of the van. "I'll send Jesse out."

"Shall I come with you?" Malcolm asked.

"I'll just tell her to look for the van and that you're not a serial rapist." Avery laughed and left Malcolm feeling uncomfortable and awkward.

The next interviewee was an attractive woman who wore a blazer and slacks and had her hair cut short, but stylishly. She reminded Malcolm of the television talk show host, Ellen, in the way she looked, her mannerisms, and her wittiness. She climbed in the van and pounced onto the futon without hesitation. After the introductions, Malcolm started the interview with the same questions.

"How do you describe yourself?"

"Bisexual," Jesse answered promptly.

"Oh. So female?" Malcolm had not questioned Jesse's sex as female. He just assumed she was lesbian.

"Yes."

"So you are attracted to both men and women?"

"Yes. Although as I've gotten older, I find men not aging well," she laughed.

"So you sleep with women primarily now?"

"I have been in a long-term relationship with a woman for the last five years."

"Could you tell me something about your past?" Malcolm didn't think that Jesse was shy, but she didn't seem to be as forthcoming as Avery was without some probing on his part.

"I spent my high school years as a sexually active heterosexual; got pregnant in fact and had an abortion in one of those seedy clinics in New York City. I fell in love with my best friend as a sophomore in college."

"You mean a woman friend?"

"Yes. But she wasn't gay, so it never developed romantically or sexually. She is still, however, my best friend and soul mate. But it awakened my lesbian side and I acted on it. In my late twenties I met a man and we married and had a son. It was a terrible marriage. He was a sociopath. But we did produce an amazing human being. I'd say I have been mostly with women since then. But I have slept with men on occasion." She smiled. "I enjoy sex . . . a lot."

She paused and Malcolm waited, thinking she would just keep talking as Avery had. Finally Malcolm spoke up. "Do you have a picture of your son?" He thought talking about him might open her up more.

"Not a recent one, but one from when he was a child." She reached into her back pocket and took out a wallet and slipped a picture out of one of the compartments. It was a picture of Jesse with a boy about eight years old. She looked completely different. Her hair was long, her clothes more feminine; she was beautiful and the picture of motherhood. It was hard to believe that this was the same woman.

"Do you mind if I take a shot of this picture?"

"No. But I would like to get it back."

"Could you hold it up for me?" Malcolm asked.

"Do you have any other questions?" Jesse asked as she held up the photo.

"Well, I guess I'd like to know how you came out to your family and if it was difficult?"

"My family was totally supportive and no, it has not been difficult for me at all. The hardest thing was coming to terms with falling in love with my friend and our conversations about it. I didn't want to lose the friendship over it."

"But you didn't?"

"No. But you asked me what was hard. That was hard. That's all."

"Thanks, Jesse. I won't keep you any longer, but can I have your number in case I have any more questions?" She gave it to him and they walked back to the club together. Malcolm figured he had time for one more interview. They paused at the door. "I'd like to talk to someone who identifies differently from Avery and you to round out the group. Do you know the other one who agreed to talk to me?" he asked.

"Lee would be a good one. I'll tell him to come over."

Jesse went to the dance floor and tapped one of the dancers on the shoulder and spoke into his ear. He looked over at Malcolm and signaled as if to say he'd be there in a minute. Malcolm could see that Lee was totally into the music, and dancing most uninhibitedly. He was not about to stop for Malcolm's sake.

The music finally stopped and Lee danced over. Malcolm assumed he was male because Jesse had referred to him that way, but he was definitely flamboyant in his mannerisms. He just looked and acted like an effeminate queen. "Well, here I am."

"Hi, Lee. I'm Malcolm."

"Hello, Malcolm," Lee purred, taking his arm. Malcolm led him to the van with some misgiving. This was perplexing. Malcolm wasn't interested in interviewing a mere homosexual man. Hopefully, Jesse knew something about

Lee that put him in the transgender or non-binary gender category. They arrived at the van and Lee primped and preened for several minutes before letting Malcolm put the camera on him.

"So what do you want to know?" Lee gushed as he settled into the futon, positioning the pillows around him as if their placement would enhance his screen presence. This was a different personality than Avery and Jesse. Lee was chatty, extroverted, and outspoken. He didn't need prompting.

"I guess I'll ask you the same questions I asked Avery and Jesse. How do you describe yourself on the gender spectrum?"

"Intersex transgender." Malcolm was surprised, having expected Lee to answer gay or female.

"Uh, can you elaborate?" Malcolm wasn't sure he knew how one could be both.

"You're doing a documentary on LGBT and you don't know what 'intersex' is?"

"I do know. It's a person born with both male and female sex characteristics."

"Then what else do you want to know?"

Malcolm finally realized that Lee was playing with him. In fact, his whole persona of the flaming queen might very well be an act for

Malcolm's benefit. "Okay," breathed Malcolm. "Let's talk about the difference between 'gender' and 'sex' as descriptive words."

"Aren't the words 'gender' and 'sex' nouns?" Lee grinned. "I do remember my English teachers always talked about adjectives being descriptive words." Lee was turning out to be a real pain in the ass.

"Since you seem to enjoy the role of professor, why don't you explain the difference between 'gender' and 'sex'?"

"Maybe it would be best to show you." Lee winked and smirked.

"This is an educational documentary so no, I don't think that would be a good idea."

"Oh dear, wouldn't want to upset the soccer moms and their perfect kiddos."

"Would you just answer my questions?"

"Fine." Lee pursed his lips. "Don't have to get snippy about it." He then raised his chin. "But you know there isn't agreement on how to define gender and sex."

"Okay, Lee. Just tell me how you interpret the difference and how it pertains to you."

"Oh goody. That's much easier. It's too hard to play sexy professor."

Malcolm smiled grimly and paused the camera. He waited while Lee repositioned the pillows and pulled his legs under him. "Are you ready now?"

"Yes. So . . . I identify male because although I am intersex and have both male and female characteristics, my dick is more prominent than my pussy." Lee gasped loudly and covered his mouth with his hand. "Oh dear, should I have used more technical terms?"

"No. That's fine." Malcolm adjusted his position and took a deep breath to hide his frustration.

"Oh, good. I like to sleep with boys, but I'm not picky about whether they're gay or straight." He smiled at Malcolm coyly. "So if you want to get together after the interview —"

"Let's stay on track, please."

"Okay. So that's my sexual orientation. As for gender identity, well, that gets a little more complicated. I don't fit into a category so I call it transgender, but it isn't really."

"What's wrong with non-binary gender?"

"Nothing. I could say that. Would you like me too?"

"I don't care what you call yourself. I'm just making a suggestion."

"Actually, non-binary sounds so 'legal' and 'bureaucratic'. Transgender sounds more flexible . . . more supple . . . more graceful."

"Then why not use gender-fluid?"

"Ooh! I like that!" Lee seemed genuinely enthusiastic. "Fluid is such a sexy word, don't you think?"

"Hey, man, call yourself whatever you want. So, you are both male and female anatomically and are attracted to men? And you identify yourself as both male and female in your, uh, social expression? Does that sound about right?"

"Social expression? How prim and proper."

"You know what I mean."

"Just trying to be PC, huh?"

"Can I ask you some other questions?"

"Ask away."

"I understand that some intersex babies were assigned one or the other sex and that doctors performed surgeries. How is it that such a surgery wasn't performed on you?"

Lee became silent and pensive. "I was lucky because I was born at home." He smiled. "Mother was a hippie."

"So your mother didn't see a doctor at all?"

"I don't know. I was kind of young at the time."

"Lee, please just answer the question," Malcolm sighed. "This is not a comedy."

"Well, I don't want to lose my chance at stardom."

Malcolm hoped Lee wouldn't take offense and walk away. He would be a fascinating and essential interview for the documentary. "She never told you anything?"

"Honestly," Lee finally continued. "I don't know. I only know she was young and naïve and poor. She probably didn't think anything was weird about my genitalia. Neither did I until I was an adolescent and started getting interested in those things. And noticed that other boys were different."

Malcolm waited for Lee to continue, but he didn't. Malcolm paused the camera. "Do you want to take a break?"

"No. I was just waiting for you to ask the next question."

"Oh. Well, honestly, I'm not sure what to ask."

"Sure you do. You're just afraid to."

"So do you use both your, uh, sexual organs when you have sex?"

"It depends on what my partner wants."

"You are, um, aroused equally, uh, with both?"

"Equally?"

"You know what I mean. Don't you?"

"They both work. Is that what you mean?"

"I guess."

"Then yes. They both work. To my satisfaction, anyway."

Malcolm took a deep breath before asking the next question. "Are you comfortable with being intersex or do you wish you were, uh, more . . . I don't know what word to use. I don't want to say 'normal'. What word do you suggest I use?"

"What's the opposite of gender fluid? Gender specific?"

"That's a good way of putting it. Did you just come up with that or do you really know all the so-called politically correct terms?"

"It doesn't really matter, does it Malcolm dear?"

"No. You're right." Malcolm smiled. "It doesn't."

Lee held up his hand. "Now, don't try to butter me up. I'm kind of done here. I'd like to get back inside. I came here to dance."

"Can I have your number if I have any more questions?"

"Sure." Lee gave Malcolm a business card.

Malcolm peered down at it and looked up at Lee with an incredulous expression. "You're a psychologist? With a PhD?"

"Why does that surprise you?"

"I won't answer until I know your consultation fee."

"Oh honey, no charge." Lee winked at him. "One never knows, do one."

"Fats Waller?" Malcolm asked.

"You a fan?"

"Isn't it a Billie Holiday song?"

"She sang it."

"One more thing. Do you prefer being called 'he'?" Malcolm asked.

"As opposed to what?"

"Well, Avery prefers 'they' and I thought in your circumstance, that would be a more appropriate pronoun."

"Hmmm. Okay. Call my dynamic duo 'they' if you prefer. I don't really care." Lee blew him a kiss and left the van.

Malcolm fell into the futon and sighed. "Wow. That was weird," he said aloud. "And uncomfortable." He sat for a few minutes, lost in thought. Finally, he got up and put the camera and lights away. He climbed into the drivers' seat. He couldn't wait to get home and show Savali what he'd videotaped.

His interview with Lee had lasted much longer than he'd realized and it was after midnight when he got home. Savali was asleep. He hooked the camera up to the television and spent most of the night watching and taking notes on how he wanted to edit it. But he wouldn't do anything until he got Savali's input. He finally fell asleep on the couch and that's where Savali found him when she got up. She took her keys out of Malcolm's pants pocket and tiptoed out of the house.

36

MALCOLM WOKE UP, NOTICED THE TIME AND HURRIED TO GET READY FOR WORK. He was excited to talk to Savali about his escapade of the previous night, but figured she had gone earlier to work out at Muscle Beach. When he got to Moss House he made a beeline for the office. He rushed in without knocking and hugged her. "Thanks for your suggestion! It was fantastic. I interviewed three people last night. I can't wait to show you."

"Glad to be of assistance. Who'd you interview?"

"I went to a Meetup in the valley. It's an LGBT group that goes dancing together. I asked who wanted to be interviewed and got three really interesting people -- all of them different from each other. One was transgender, one was bisexual, and one was intersex. I have them on tape. Will you wait up for me tonight? Ill try to leave work early."

"Aye, aye, sir. If I'm asleep when you get home, you can wake me up. I give you permission."

Malcolm kissed her and left the office, grinning from ear to ear. "What are you so happy about?" George grumbled as he passed Malcolm.

"My documentary is coming together. I have some great footage."

"Good for you." George smiled weakly, the best he could muster.

Malcolm breezed through the afternoon and evening, hugging everyone at Moss House as he helped them and dancing around his tables at Café Gratitude. His cheerfulness was contagious, and his tips were plentiful. He asked to be the first one off, so Savali was lying on the living room couch, watching a movie, when he got home. "Wow. You're home early," she said.

"I made great tips tonight so I asked to get off as soon as the dinner rush was over. Do you need to finish watching this movie or can I plug my camera into the TV?"

Savali cocked her head and gave him a half smile. "Go ahead. It's Netflix. I can watch the end another time."

He set up the camera and sat down next to her on the sofa. "I haven't edited yet or anything, and I got everyone's number if I need to do any follow up." Avery came up on the screen. "That's Avery. She's female but wants to be called 'they' so —"

"Hey, Malcolm," Savali interrupted. "Just let me watch without any commentary."

"Okay." Malcolm settled into the sofa and put his arm around her. Savali nestled up to him and together they watched without talking.

"This is great, Malcolm. This really completes the picture we are trying to present that there are many sides to gender and sexuality."

But that was only the beginning of their collaboration. There were as many arguments as agreements. Savali felt that she was more knowledgeable on the subject and Malcolm had particular points he wanted to make with the film. They had to do a great deal of compromising, which added a lot of time to the development stage. It was finally written and ready to shoot two months later. They had managed to raise a few thousand dollars, but they needed at least a hundred thousand more to get it made.

As soon as Savali had agreed to the documentary, Malcolm set up a GoFundMe that had quickly received a trickle of donations.

A number of residents of Moss House had all contributed what they could, and Malcolm had decided to use the savings he had set aside for the car for the movie, but it was still far short. He was starting to feel a little discouraged, but he went ahead anyway, setting up what he could with what they had.

Malcolm got home one afternoon when he had the night off. Savali sat at the dining room table waiting for him, a bottle of champagne and two glasses on the table in front of her. She grinned and said, "Sit down and prepare to be blown away."

He looked at her warily but grinned back. "Okay." He sat down as Savali popped the cork and poured the champagne into the glasses.

They clicked glasses as she said, "A toast to Nick." She took a sip, but Malcolm held his glass up and didn't move. "Go ahead, take a sip."

He took a small sip. "Did you hear from him? He's okay?"

"Oh, he's more than okay. No, I didn't hear from him, but you did."

"Huh?"

She took a postcard off her lap and handed it to him. The picture was of the island of Ischia, off the coast of Italy. Malcolm looked at the picture and then turned it over. "Take the road less traveled and it'll make all the difference. Nick." Savali took her laptop that was sitting on the table and opened it. She swung the screen over so Malcolm could see. It was his GoFundMe site and the goal of $120,000 had been reached. "Apparently, Nick came into some money and wanted to pay you back!"

He jumped up and hugged and kissed her. "Oh my God! It's really happening!" Then he sat down and got contemplative. "Do we care where the money is coming from?"

"What do you mean? Of course not! Maybe it is illegal drug money, but who cares? Anyway, it's not like we know where anyone else's money comes from."

"Guess so." He exhaled loudly and then gulped down the rest of his champagne. He poured some more and toasted her again. "This is amazing." He picked up the card and turned it over and over. "No address to thank him."

"Oh Malcolm, don't be a dumbfuck. Of course he's not going to write his address on a postcard."

"Oh yeah, right. Anyway, apparently he knows what we're doing, so he'll keep in touch from time to time, I hope. Well, I guess we should go out for dinner to celebrate," Malcolm added, but not with much enthusiasm. He was itching to start on the film right away.

"Nah, I already took care of that. Remember when I promised to cook you a rocking dinner? I figured tonight was the perfect night."

"Awesome, another great surprise," Malcolm said. "I bet it will be delicious."

"You're damn right."

Savali made a balsamic-glazed salmon with saffron rice and a kale salad. When they were finishing up, she asked, "Are you going to be able to do this and keep two jobs and two volunteering activities?"

Malcolm frowned. "No. But I'm not sure what to give up."

"Yes you are."

"Care to share with me since you seem to know?"

"You make much more at the cafe and you don't want to let down the kids at the hospital. Charlie's been training the homeless to take care of the table and, honestly, the residents can handle the morning activities. I thought maybe we'd both use the mornings to work on the film, and then you could work afternoons at Moss House and evenings at the cafe. I'll ask Annabel to switch my hours to afternoon and evening."

"You mean I'm not indispensable?"

"Nope, you're not."

"So you've thought this all out." He smiled and took her hand. "You're into this too."

"It's my life. Of course I'm into it."

"But I meant, you're excited about it?"

"Is that a question?"

"Yes. It seems that you are, but you aren't an easy person to figure out."

"And that's the way I like it. I like being an enigma."

"I know."

They stayed up most of the night strategizing. They spoke to Annabel who was fine with the new schedule. The residents quickly adjusted to running the morning activities themselves, and enthusiasm over the project spread beyond Finn. Things were working out perfectly.

Malcolm finished the editing process and made the trailer. A couple of months later they were ready to look for distribution. He spent a lot of time making calls and going to meetings, hitting up all his old contacts and any new ones he could find. He and Savali barely saw each other except for their nights in bed, and he was usually exhausted and only interested in sleeping.

He had a meeting with a potential distributor one evening and got the go-ahead. He was ecstatic and couldn't wait to share the news with Savali, but she was not home when he got there. That was strange. She probably had to work late at Moss House. He waited up until midnight, calling and texting her, and finally went to bed without hearing a word back from her.

He slept fitfully, checking the time continually. He finally got up at dawn, unable to get to sleep. He was in the kitchen making coffee when the front door opened and Savali entered. She was dressed like a preppy in slacks, a button-down shirt, and a sports jacket. "Well, that's an interesting outfit," Malcolm said coldly. "Where've you been?"

Savali stared at him and then looked away. "I'm sorry."

"Sorry for?"

"I don't know. What should I be sorry for?" she answered.

"Well, how about starting with not answering my calls and texts."

"Okay. We can start with that."

"What are you getting at Savali? Is there something else you should be sorry for?"

"No. I mean, you might think so. But I don't."

"What the hell is that supposed to mean?"

She leaned against the kitchen counter and took a deep breath. "I went to a singles bar last night and went home with a woman."

"You what?" Malcolm started pacing back and forth in the kitchen. Then he went into the living room and plopped down on the sofa.

She followed him and sat in the chair across from him. "I needed to."

"You needed to? You needed to have sex with a woman? What the hell, Savali!"

"I thought you would understand who I am after making the film."

"I get who you are, but does that mean that you have to act on every impulse? I haven't. Don't you think that I have wanted to sleep with a woman too?"

"I've never stopped you. That's your hang-up."

"So what you're saying is that if we stay together as a couple, we can sleep with whoever we want when the mood hits us?"

"Yes."

"Well, I don't think I want that."

"So, what do you want?" Savali asked, taking his hand.

He pulled his hand away. "I don't know. But this doesn't feel good at all." They sat in silence for a few minutes and then Malcolm added, "And by the way, I got a distributor last night. I was eager to share the good news with you, but I guess that's not important to you."

"That's wonderful. And it is important to me. But being who I am is also important."

Malcolm stood up and opened his mouth to speak, then thought it better not to and walked out.

37

SAVALI PACKED HER THINGS AND MOVED BACK INTO HER VAN. Malcolm didn't try to stop her, although he wasn't sure how he felt. He managed to keep himself busy working with the distributor and taking on any extra hours he could at the cafe. He and Savali kept their distance at work. She hid out in her office when he was around, and they only nodded in passing or when they got stuck in a situation together. Most of the residents knew something was up, but only talked about it among themselves.

Finn was the only person to ask Malcolm what was going on. He tried to remain neutral while allowing Malcolm to vent, but he also understood Savali's point of view. One day, Malcolm was having an especially hard time. He missed Savali's input on the film as well as her body in his bed. "You look like you haven't slept all night."

Malcolm shrugged. "I guess I didn't sleep much."

"Maybe it would help to talk to her."

"And say what? I don't know what to say. I don't know what I feel or what I want."

"You do know what you want, but you can't have it that way."

"What I want is to have fallen in love with a woman, not a man."

"Well, that's not what happened, Malcolm," Finn sighed. "And I dare say it makes you appear juvenile after all the screwing you've done. The real issue is that you can't come to terms with Savali cheating on you. No matter what your gender or sexual identity, that's pretty much the universal reaction when the person you love hurts you."

"She doesn't consider it cheating on me. She just keeps coming back to that's who she is and I need to just accept it."

"No, Malcolm. You don't have to accept it, even when you accept her as a person of non-binary gender. Did I get the politically correct title for her right?"

"I think that's the latest PC one." Malcolm sighed.

"What I'm trying to say is that her identity is not based on who she sleeps or doesn't sleep with. It's simply her choice at the moment — to act on impulse or not. The key word, Malcolm, is choice . . . for both of you. Have you asked her?"

"Asked her what?"

"If she's willing to make the choice not to act on it."

"No, because she said that I needed to accept her and that sleeping with others is part of her."

"Just saying, Malcolm. Maybe you can try talking to her about what I said. You might be surprised."

Malcolm was quiet for a minute. "Have you talked to her about any of this?" he finally asked.

"No. She isn't sharing any of this with me. And I would never tell her anything you and I have talked about."

"I know you wouldn't. I just thought maybe she talked to you about how she felt."

"Well, even if she had, I wouldn't tell you."

As the documentary's release drew near, Malcolm and Savali had to have some discussion on several things. The conversation was cordial and formal, even when they disagreed on the details. Neither of them wanted to rock the boat and possibly postpone its release so it was a good exercise in listening to each other and resolving differences. Even so, Malcolm had resigned himself to the fact that he would probably quit Moss House after the film came out. He didn't think he could move on if he had to see Savali every day.

Finally, it was the night of the opening at an independent theater in West Hollywood. Violet had glued herself to Finn as her date for the event, while Finn had invited Martin and his son, Michael, and daughter-in-law, Carla to temper her behavior a bit. Kate, of course, was in Africa. Malcolm had invited Jed and Monica, but they were unable to make it. They promised to see it when it came to San Francisco.

Savali and Malcolm spoke together to the audience about the making of the film. The place was packed with members of the LGBT community and the alternative press, as well as Malcolm's friends from the cafe, the boardwalk, the homeless resource center, and the hospital. The film got a standing ovation.

There was a party afterward put on by the distributor, and the elation from the film's success overshadowed any impasse between Malcolm and Savali. They managed to stay away from each other as much as possible, which wasn't hard. The LGBT community swarmed around Savali, asking her to give presentations at various meetings and workshops. The press kept Malcolm busy along with the distributor's film industry connections. Malcolm's and Savali's friends didn't get much of an opportunity to squeeze in more than a hug or handshake with either of them.

When the party was over and the guests had left, Malcolm and the distributor met for a while to discuss the next steps. It was after midnight when Malcolm left the theater. He had called Uber for a ride and stood in front of the theater, waiting for his ride to show up. Savali's van drove up and she opened the passenger side door. "Can I drive you home?"

Malcolm wanted to get in and be with her, but he thought better of it. "I've got an Uber ride coming."

"C'mon. Let's talk. Please."

He got in. "Why?"

"Because we need to."

"I don't want to. Not yet."

"I love you, Malcolm. And no matter what happens, I always will. I just wanted to tell you that."

Just then a car drove up. "That's my ride." Malcolm got out of the van. He got into the car and gave his address to the driver.

"Hey, that's not too far from my house," the driver said as she drove off. "How convenient since you're my last call."

Malcolm looked at the driver and noticed that she was a pretty, young woman about his age. They talked all the way to Malcolm's house. She was an aspiring actress so she enjoyed hearing about Malcolm's filmmaking. When they got to his house, he ended up inviting her in, and after finishing a bottle of wine, they ended up in Malcolm's bed.

It was awkward the next morning, and she got up hurriedly and left, claiming she was late for an audition. Malcolm, meanwhile, stayed in bed pondering the entire night. A lot had happened, and his emotions seesawed from euphoria over the success of the movie and the enjoyment of sex with a biological woman, to despondency over Savali. Luckily, it was Sunday, and he had asked for the night off from the cafe.

He stayed home the whole day, not showering or eating. He was as confused as he ever was, and now that the movie was finished, he was back to not having a particular direction.

At least he knew he wanted to keep making films, and he thought Homer and the wonders of music, dancing, and boxing for the treatment of Parkinson's would be his next subject.

Finally at about four, he decided he needed to go grocery shopping, so he took a shower and was getting dressed when there was a knock at the front door. He opened it and there was Savali, dressed in those same clothes that had blown him away many months before when he first saw her dressed as a female on her date with Byron. "I called the cafe and they said you had the night off. Can we have dinner?"

He couldn't take his eyes off her and he couldn't ignore the feelings rising in him. "Oh, Savali . . ."

"Please. Just dinner."

He sighed. "Oh fine. Let me change my clothes."

"Can I watch?" she giggled. He didn't answer and went back to the bedroom to change. "Just trying to lighten the mood," she called out to him.

They went to the Ale House, for old times sake, and talked about the film. Malcolm caught her up with the houses it was going to be shown in around the country. "And it's slated for a few film festivals."

"What are you going to do next?" she asked.

"I'm thinking Homer and Parkinson's and how music steadies his tremors. "

"Sounds good."

They were silent for a minute, sipping their beers and finishing their meals. "I slept with my Uber driver last night," he blurted out.

Savali laughed. "Well, that's interesting. Male or female?"

"For God's sake, Savali. You know it was a woman."

"I know. Just checking to see if I'm rubbing off on you," she laughed. And then earnestly, "So, how was it?"

"It was nice."

She didn't say anything for a minute. "Is that what you want, then?"

"Yes. And no."

"Hmm. What does that mean?"

"I think it means that I want to be with you and sleep with women every now and then."

Savali beamed and took his hands. "So, we're good?"

"For now, anyway."

"We can just let it unfold?"

"I guess that's what I'm saying. I'm not sure. But I do know that I miss you and want to be with you."

"I've missed you too, Malcolm."

They gazed into each other's eyes and held hands. "And maybe . . . "

Savali cocked her head, waiting for him to finish. Finally she said, "Maybe what?"

Malcolm took a breath. "Maybe we won't want to sleep with others."

Savali glanced away. "I don't know that I can change that desire."

"Well . . . if we do, maybe we don't have to act on the impulse."

Now Savali was silent for a minute. "Maybe." Malcolm leaned over the table and kissed her. "No promises . . . yet," she added. "But I will think about that. I don't ever want to hurt you again."

"Let's just see what happens. We can play it by ear."

"You know, Malcolm, I'd also like to have children someday . . . just so you know."

Malcolm grinned.

Acknowledgements:

First and foremost I want to thank Daniel Nauman who edited, critiqued, advised, and encouraged in every aspect of the writing and publishing.

Glenn Tucker for producing the audiobook and also helping me create videos and the music to accompany them.

Raechel Mullen for her incredible cover.

Chris Saur for his editing and advising.

Andy Hanson, Kris Kidd, and David Gallo for their critiques.

And Tin Roof Café for providing my favorite place to write.

Emily Gallo lives in Chico, California and Carpinteria, California with her husband, David, and their Schillerhound, Gracie. *Roads Not Taken* is her fourth novel.

Read an excerpt from Emily's fifth novel:
MURDER AT THE COLUMBARIUM:

IT SOUNDED LIKE A CAT IN DISTRESS, MEOWING LOUDLY IN THE BUSHES. Jed was just unlocking the front gate of the columbarium to open for the day. It wouldn't be the first time a cat had found its home in the bushes of the columbarium. Word must have gotten out to the San Francisco cat population that Jed was a soft touch and always had a supply of food handy. When he stooped to look, however, he found a pink blanket swaddling a baby who looked to be only a couple of months old. As he brushed the branches away to lift the baby, he noticed a black shoe a few inches away from a leg and then the body of a woman. She wore a long dress, the skirt of which was up, wrapped around her neck. She had a hijab covering her head so that her face was exposed. Her eyes were open but stared straight ahead, vacantly. Jed stood frozen, holding the screaming infant in his arms. Finally, he pulled himself together enough to rock and shush the baby and walk away.

He brought the baby into the office and sat down at his desk. He wished he had a rocking chair but he thought he could use the office chair as a substitute. Maybe a swivel action could work similarly to the rocking motion that always worked well at Miss Ruthie's in Venice and at the hospital just down the street. Jed wasn't new to soothing babies in pain so he was good at it. His brain scanned through his limited repertoire of songs to come up with an appropriate one and landed on *Amazing Grace*. Maybe that one was too appropriate.

After quieting the baby, Jed came to his senses and realized he needed to call the police. His past experiences with police had not been positive, but hopefully enough years had passed so none of that would come up. He dialed 911.

"I am the caretaker of the columbarium on Lorraine Court and I just got to work. I found a dead body on the grounds . . . and a baby lying next to it." He took a deep breath. It had been a long time since he needed to use his pranayama breathing. "Yes. The baby is alive. Uh, Jed Gibbons. Okay. I won't touch the body." He hung up and continued to breathe and rock the baby until he heard the distant sound of sirens. Then he stood up and walked outside.